The Secret Life of Hodge, the Bookstore Cat

AT

SELECTED WORKS USED BOOKS AND SHEET MUSIC

IN THE FINE ARTS BUILDING IN DOWNTOWN CHICAGO

Suzanne Erfurth

with illustrations by

Beatriz E. Ledesma

ISBN-13: 978-0692594025 (Custom Universal)
ISBN-10: 0692594027

I am Hodge, and I endorse this true and authentic account of my fictional secret life and memoirs.

Hodge, when he's got the time, stalls out and gives this look that shouts, "WHAT? What is it, man? What now?" You really want to apologize...offer him something. Then he takes off to points unknown as if to whisper, "Please," while calling you a few names under his breath...leaves you looking around... wondering...where is he...where is he?

—Jeff McNary, who, along with Keith Peterson, Peterson's bookstore in downtown Chicago, and Peterson's wife and cats, really exists. Otherwise, this is a work of fiction, though Hodge may tell you otherwise.

BL

OCTOBER

Hodge Spots a Leopard

"Do you have *Bengal Cats: A Complete Pet Owner's Manual*?" asked a customer.

"Let me check," said Keith, and returned shortly from another room in the store with the book in his hand.

Hodge, hearing the word "cat," came over and hopped up on Keith's desk to investigate.

"'Pet'? 'Owner'?" he said to the customer. "You seem to be unclear on the concept of hosting a cat, sister." Hodge sometimes forgot that humans rarely understand cat speech.

"Nice kitty," said the customer, scratching him behind his ears. "I love cats."

Ignoring her, Hodge examined the book cover. His eyes widened.

"What a magnificent creature," he miaowed, half to Keith and half to himself. "Look at those spots! And the big rounded ears, and the black outline around his eyes, like he's wearing mascara. Boss Man, we need one of these cats here in the store. It gets lonely at night. I need a companion who's up to my standard. You know, brilliant, beautiful, athletic?"

The humans, uncomprehending, continued their conversation above him.

"I'm hoping it has some advice on how to deal with kitty angst," said the customer as she rummaged for her wallet in her purse. "I adopted a Bengal from a breed rescue society. I take him out on walks in his leash and harness so he doesn't get bored, but lately he's been too skittish and fearful to enjoy it much. The neighbors' new dog scares him, and whenever he sees, like, even a little half-grown alley cat, he puffs up and starts hissing like it's some big territorial threat."

"Good luck," said Keith as she paid him and he put the book in a bag for her, which involved removing it from under Hodge's paw.

As the doors closed behind the customer, Hodge walked across the desk to the computer keyboard, used his nose and paws to start a YouTube recording of "Yesterday," and then began to type. After a few minutes he stepped back and revealed the screen, which now read:

Lullaby for a Bengal Cat

Rounded Ears,
You are efficacious as three beers,
But my Bengal has unfounded fears.
Oh calm yourself, my Rounded Ears.
[Bridge]
No, that alley cat won't attack. He wants to play.
You are all puffed up and have frightened him
Away…

Rounded Ears,
I'll be with you through the years.
My affections won't be in arrears,
So please chill out, my Rounded Ears.

Keith read the short lyric. "Hodge," he said, "this is amazing."

"Good grief, he knows I write song parodies," muttered Hodge irritably to himself. "I've been doing it for a year—"

"This is the first time I've ever seen you express actual affectionate concern and genuine empathy for anyone else's feelings," continued Keith. "It's completely out of character. H'm…maybe the only people

"I've been doing it for a year—"

you care about are exotic-looking cats? You have a thing about our cat at home, Ma'at—"

"STOP!" howled Hodge, puffing up and laying his ears back. "My private life is my business. Besides, I didn't tell you you could mention her name to me!"

"Hodge, who do you think you are?" demanded Keith, irritably and rhetorically.

"Mayor Emanuel," responded Hodge instantly, stretching out luxuriously on the desk. "L' état, c'est moi. I'm taking a nap."

"L' état, c'est moi."

NOVEMBER

Hodge, the Great Healer

A young man emerged from the vintage Victorian elevator into the second floor hallway of the Fine Arts Building, nodded pleasantly to the impassive elevator attendant, and wove his way unsteadily toward the bookstore, then struggled briefly with the door before realizing it opened outward. "Hey," he said to Keith, cheerfully and rather loudly, "I see you have sheet music. My girlfriend sent me out to look for a song by Leonard Cohen but I can't remember the name of it. It's really depressing."

"That doesn't exactly narrow the field," pointed out Hodge.

"Nice kitty," said the customer. "All I know is that everybody and his brother has recorded it, and it's kind of slow and melancholy and has arpeggios. I ended up stopping by Miller's Pub, just to grab an early lunch and cheer up, after she played it for me on the guitar this morning. I stayed there drinking and watching the game for seven hours. Anyone want the rest of my fish sandwich?"

"Hallelujah!" exclaimed Hodge, pouncing on the paper bag the customer was waving in the air, and carrying it away in his teeth. Before

Keith could stop him he had jumped up into the rafters and begun tearing through the foil wrapping.

"My advice to you," Hodge miaowed down to the customer through a mouthful of deep-fried cod fillet, "is to go check out the sheet music section in the next room, and find something upbeat that people can sing along with; dump that chick before she dumps you; and head back to the bar and find someone nice to watch the game with. And next time could you bring extra tartar sauce?"

• •

"Do you have any books on the Healing Gaze?" asked a customer, threading her way through the increasingly crowded bookstore at the Fine Arts Building's monthly open studios reception, and politely refusing a glass of wine.

"No," said Keith and Hodge more or less in chorus, Keith politely and Hodge derisively. "Nice kitty," observed the customer. "Cats are magic."

"Watch me do a magic trick," said Hodge, reaching unceremoniously into a bowl of potato chips that Keith had put out for the customers, and managing to grab a mouthful.

"Get out of that," exclaimed Keith, removing Hodge from the table.

The door opened. Hodge darted toward it, muttering "Call me Houdini," but the pair of customers slipped quickly into the store and closed the door behind them before he could escape. Keith and Hodge recognized the young man, but not his friend.

"You were here looking for sheet music for 'Hallelujah' a week ago—Leonard Cohen, not Handel," said Keith, as Hodge exclaimed ecstatically, "You gave me half a fish sandwich from Miller's Pub! Got another?"

"Right," said the customer, accepting a glass of wine and draining it. "This is my girlfriend Mindy." The young woman shook Keith's hand. "I'm not the one who sent him out in the cold looking for sheet music," she explained.

"We met at a piano bar that same evening I was here," said the customer. "When I couldn't remember the name of the song—"

"I told you *that,*" interrupted Hodge, "though I was primarily reacting to the sandwich. Do you have any more?"

"Nice kitty," continued the customer. "Anyway, I went around the corner into that room over there and picked up a Beatles anthology, and bought it and took it to the bar, and Mindy and I bonded somewhere during the chorus of 'Hey Jude.' Elaine told me she was trying to figure out a way to end our relationship anyway."

"Congratulations," said Keith, briefly wondering whether there was a way to discourage the otherwise pleasant young man from over-sharing, and quickly deciding that there wasn't—and recalling some past gatherings in the store that made the youth seem like a model of discretion.

"It's funny, I somehow realized things were going to change when I was looking up into the rafters at your cat and he was miaowing down at me," said the young man. "I knew what to do, all of a sudden, and that everything would be all right."

"You just did what I told you to, except that you seem to have forgotten to bring me another sandwich and extra tartar sauce, you idiot," said Hodge. "Although...I keep forgetting that humans don't always understand spoken cat, so maybe there's more to it than that. Maybe I have the Healing Gaze? I can try it on other people." He hopped up onto the desk, walked over to Keith, and stared deeply into his eyes.

"You've BEEN fed," said Keith. "Move."

Undeterred, Hodge proceeded into the middle room where the vintage mysteries were, jumped up onto the top of a small ladder, and stared fixedly at a man who was deeply absorbed in Michael Innes's *Lament for a Maker.* The man looked up, slowly, disoriented and suddenly self-conscious, finally focusing on Hodge.

"That cat is creeping me out," he announced to no one in particular, heading with the book to the cash register.

Hodge retreated toward the window, where a trio of pigeons had settled in to roost on the ledge for the evening. He gazed at them long and steadily. One of them saw him out of the corner of its eye, and all three flew off in a confused flurry of feathers, cooing and guano.

"The Healing Gaze apparently only works on people who know they have a problem and want to change," decided Hodge.

All three flew off in a confused flurry of feathers, cooing and guano.

DECEMBER

Rodents of Unusual Size

Hodge was alone in the bookstore while Keith, half a mile away in the Chicago Loop, was stuck in an apparently endless line at the Post Office two weeks before Christmas. Suddenly a movement on top of a bookcase caught Hodge's eye. Without thinking, he jumped from a perch in the lower rafters and landed with his paws on either side of what he realized was a very juvenile mouse.

"Help!" it squeaked.

"Will you chill out?" demanded Hodge. "I don't eat mice. I didn't even know you were one. I just jumped down here out of pure instinct when I saw you move."

"But my mother said all cats eat mice. And she said she heard the Boss Man telling you to 'do something about her' when he saw her last summer."

"As Lou Reed very sensibly pointed out, you can't always trust your mother," admonished Hodge. "And when did your mother ever see me do what the Boss Man told me to?"

"I'm scared," chittered the mouse.

"Kid," said Hodge, "you need to stop seeing me as a threat. And furthermore, you need some confidence-building exercises. Did you know," he said, warming to his theme, "that paleontologists recently discovered a fossilized rodent the size of a buffalo in South America? You're descended from giants. Here, let me give you a seasonal history lesson."

Hodge leaped gracefully onto the big, old desk and over to the computer, activated a YouTube video of Christmas music from the New York Philharmonic with his nose and paws, and began typing expertly with these on the computer keyboard. The mouse watched from a safe distance, looking nervously from Hodge's behind to the door in case Keith came back unexpectedly. Hodge took a while to finish, but eventually stepped aside and invited the mouse to read what was on the screen.

The mouse skittered down the bookcase and hopped onto the desk. It stared at the screen for a long time, and finally admitted, in a very small voice, "I think that's above my reading level."

"Then I'll sing it," said Hodge. "It goes to the tune of 'Angels We Have Heard on High'—"

Rodents of unusual size
Sweetly grazing on the plains.
Capybara magnified,
Munching peaceably his grains.

NU-UUUUU-UUUUU-UUUUU-TRIA,
See your giant forebear,
NU-UUUUU-UUUUU-UUUUU-TRIA,
Heading for the wa-aa-ter.

Crafty condor overhead,
Circling the pristine sky,
Calculates the size ratio:
This is someone not to try.

NU-UUUUU-UUUUU-UUUUU-TRIA,
Scientists inform us,
NU-UUUUU-UUUUU-UUUUU-TRIA,
Grandpa was eno-or-mous.

Housecat sets his sights upon
Unsuspecting guinea pig,
Just as once a sabre-tooth
Contemplated something big.
But, alert, the Cavalry
Grabs him by his furry scruff,
Dumps him roughly out the door,
Muttering, "Enough's enough."

NU-UUUUU-UUUUU-UUUUU-TRIA,
Grandpa had good flavor,
NU-UUUUU-UUUUU-UUUUU-TRIA,
But, alas, no savior.

"See?" he said triumphantly to the mouse. "Wait—NOW where are you going? I told you I don't eat mice."

"I actually believe you, but look what's coming down the hall," said the mouse.

"It's just the Boss Man," said Hodge.

"But look at his face," said the mouse. "See you later!"

Keith opened the door, his expression suggesting a cross between Heathcliff and Banquo's ghost at the feast.

"OK," miaowed Hodge to the uncomprehending Keith. "I get it. You've been at the Post Office for over an hour and are thinking about the Federal Government again. Nap time for Hodge." He jumped up onto the highest rafter and vanished discreetly from view.

• •

Hodge was napping in a chair in the front room of the bookstore, after expending all his energies harassing the pigeons outside the window, when he was awakened by someone pulling on his tail. "What," he yawned, "is the meaning of this outrage?" But when he opened his eyes, he found that the offender wasn't some literate yob but the young mouse he had been talking to a few days earlier.

"Oh, it's you," he said indulgently. "What's up, kid?"

"Oh good," said the mouse. "I didn't know if you were going to wake

"It's just the Boss Man."

up. I've been pulling your tail for ten minutes."

"You don't know how lucky you are," mused Hodge. "Do me a favor: don't try that with anyone else or you'll end up as crunchy cat food before you know what's happened to you."

"Oh, I wouldn't," the mouse assured him. "I'm afraid of everyone but you. I woke you up because I needed to talk to you. I'm being bullied in the woodwork, and I'm too scared to fight back. I was wondering if you could sing me another song about how our rodent ancestors were big and dangerous. It made me feel brave."

"Fortunately for you, kid, giant rodent fossils have been in the news a lot lately," said Hodge. "It turns out that the one I was telling you about isn't even the biggest one they've found so far. That was P. Pattersonii. They found Josephoartigasia monesi later and he's even bigger. Follow me and I'll tell you about him as soon as we can get some time on the computer without the Boss Man noticing you." Hodge jumped down to the floor and proceeded around the corner toward the desk, with the mouse following at a safe distance, to find Keith pulling on his coat and reaching in his pocket for his keys.

"I'm heading out for half an hour to pick up provisions for the Second Fridays open studios reception. This month it's the big holiday one," Keith told Hodge. "Just breathe deeply and try to stay calm; I'll be back before you know it," he added sarcastically as Hodge turned his back on him in an elaborate parody of indifference. Sensing, mistakenly, that Hodge was plotting to wheel about and escape through the open door as usual, he slipped out quickly and locked it behind him.

"The coast is clear," called Hodge to the mouse. "Come on out. " He hopped up onto the desk and activated a YouTube video of the Robert Shaw Chorale singing "O Come All Ye Faithful."

"This is a march," he told the mouse. "Mice don't march and cats certainly don't either, but marching music is good for getting your courage up. If you need to. I've never been afraid of anything except missing dinner." He began to type with his nose and paws. After a while he hit the Save button and motioned the mouse over to the screen with his tail.

"Check that out," he said. "Oh, wait, I forget you're still learning how to read. I'll sing it for you."

O come, giant rodents,
Prehistoric mammals,
Come, let us contemplate your enormous size.
P. Pattersoni,
You have been outclassed by
Josephoartigasia
Josephoartigasia
Josephoartigasia mo-o-nesi.

On a scale model
Any capybara
Standing beside you would look like a shrew;
And as a house pet
You would need a carport,
Josephoartigasia
Josephoartigasia
Josephoartigasia mo-o-nesi.

He began to type with his nose and paws.

If you could swallow
Humans and disgorge them,
More or less unscathed, you could get a gig:
Used as a bus you'd solve our transit crisis,
Josephoartigasia
Josephoartigasia
Josephoartigasia mo-o-nesi.

"I'm the size of a bus!" chortled the mouse. "No one can hurt me. I'm too big. I can roll right over anyone who gets in my way. Whee!"

"I think you're unclear on the concept," sighed Hodge. "It isn't my fault that they don't teach evolution in the primary grades—hey, I see the Boss Man coming. You'd better skedaddle."

"No way!" squeaked the mouse. "I'll swallow him and dis-, dis-..."

Keith opened the door. Hodge jumped to the floor and feinted an escape attempt to divert Keith's attention, but Keith was too quick for him, and the door closed with the cat still in the store—and the mouse making itself at home on Keith's mouse pad and staring insolently up at him.

"I can explain—" began Hodge.

"Hodge, why don't you learn to hunt something that isn't either me or outside of the window pane?" demanded Keith. "It isn't exactly rocket science." He reached out with a gloved hand to grab the mouse, but Hodge was quicker and intercepted him, grabbing the thick leather glove with his teeth and claws, and swinging acrobatically from Keith's arm while beginning to purr. The mouse just stared. Hodge dropped down on the desk, grabbed the mouse by the scruff of its tiny neck, and leaped onto a high bookshelf, where he disappeared from view and negotiated his way down to the floor behind the books.

"You've had enough excitement for one day," he told the mouse. "Go home. We have a party to get ready for—it's Open Studios, and while I am the last person to admit to prejudice of any kind, I can confidently predict that mice will be PNG." The mouse caught its breath, looked disoriented, and skittered back into a small hole in the woodwork.

"Mission accomplished, Chief," Hodge told Keith, returning to the desk and curling up on it, while licking his lips suggestively and looking sated. Keith scratched him behind his ears, and began putting out wine and potato chips for the Second Fridays crowd—and none too soon, since the building and the store were beginning to fill with people. Hodge curled up in his cat bed and welcomed the stream of guests at the bookstore with his usual stare, resolving to count how many times someone looked at him and said "Nice kitty," and hoping that he could present the data to Keith later, in a typed note, as evidence of his need for a discreet skull and crossbones charm to attach to his collar, "just for these special occasions."

"Do you have any books on food sanitation?" asked a customer, reaching a large, grimy paw into the bowl of potato chips. "My son is training to be a chef and I gather it's an important part of the gig—what the…?" He broke off and pointed to the bowl, in which a very small mouse was nibbling at a large, curly chip and staring defiantly up at him.

"HODGE!" exclaimed Keith, but Hodge was already out of his cat bed and on the table, once again grabbing the mouse and disappearing with him into the rafters.

"Sorry about that," said Keith.

"I'll keep quiet about it or everybody will want one," quipped the customer.

"Fawlty Towers!" recognized Keith joyfully, refilling the customer's wine glass with an unusually heavy pour, and dumping the potato chips into the wastebasket. He found another, clean bowl and refilled that. "Your cat's a fine mouser," added the customer, "and such a nice kitty, too."

In the southeast corner of the store, away from the activity by the entrance, Hodge put the mouse down next to a crack in the wall just above the floorboards. "That," he told the mouse, "is a secret passage to the paperweight gallery next door. They are likely to be very busy, and to have some really good cheeses. But unless you're very careful and no one sees you, you won't get any cheese, and someone will see you and catch you and trap you forever in a glass paperweight. Got it?"

"Yes, Mr. Cat," said the mouse, looking worried again, but twitching its nose in delight as it caught the aroma of aged Cheddar through the crack in the wall. "I'll be careful. Have a nice party." It slipped through the crack and into the next room.

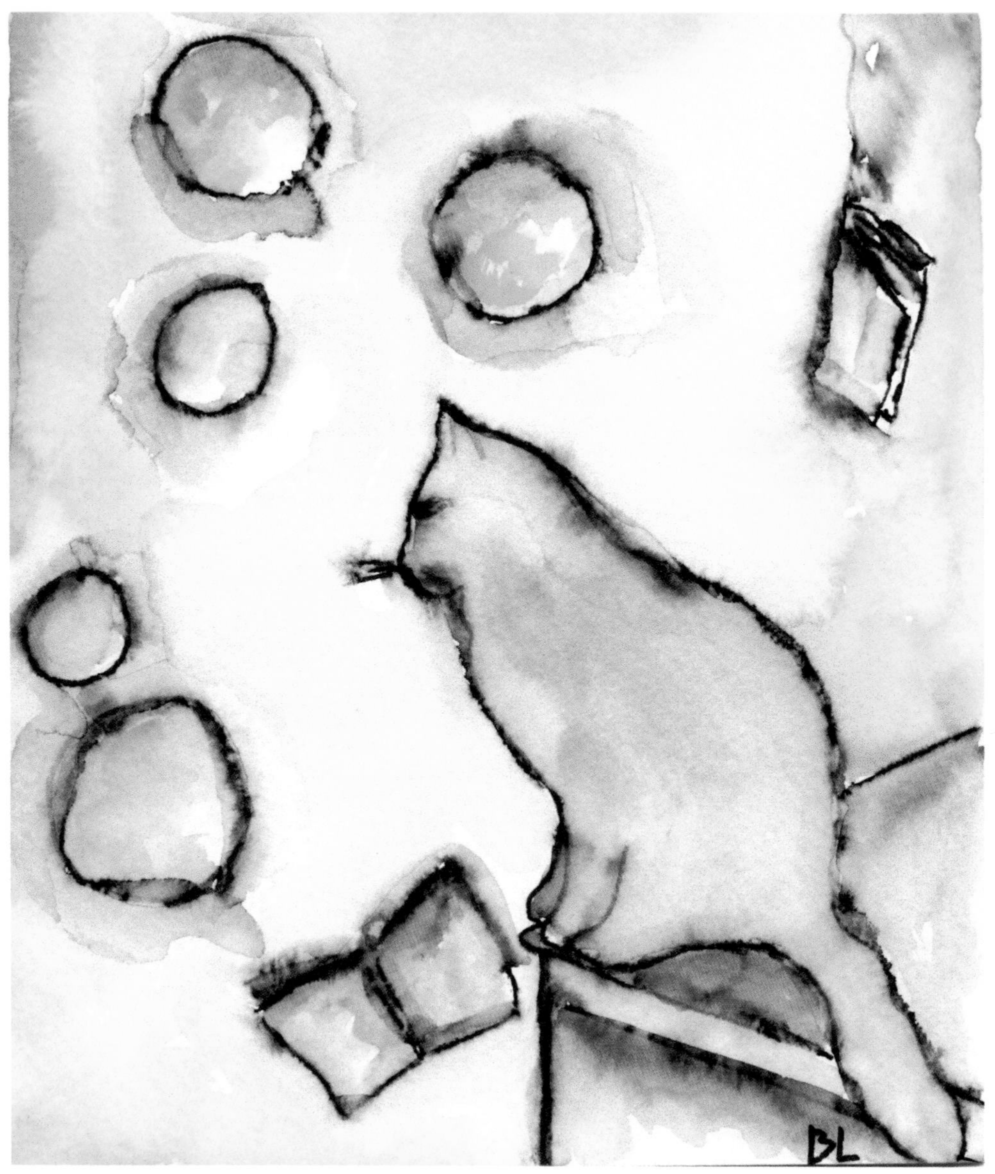

"A secret passage to the paperweight gallery next door."

"I just hope he doesn't wander over and start looking at the nature paperweights with the frogs and butterflies—he won't know they're glass and he'll think he's stumbled on a serial killer," Hodge muttered. "Although he's so ignorant he probably won't even recognize the animal images. Anyway, I'm out of the guidance counseling business from this day forward." He returned to the desk, and found that the press of customers was so dense that it was safest to hide somewhere where no one could step on his tail.

An hour later there was a brief lull, and Keith was able to relax for a moment.

"What's that rhythmic crunching sound?" asked a customer. "It's like some sort of avant-garde solo percussion instrument."

"It seems to be coming from the trashcan," said another customer.

Keith leaned over and peered into the depths of the gray wastebasket with its gray plastic bin liner, then reached in and pulled out his gray cat, whose belly was now distended after eating a quart of discarded potato chips.

"Hide in plain sight," explained Hodge dreamily as he waddled into his cat bed. "Nap time. Catch you later."

A quart of discarded potato chips.

BL

"A particular paperweight that I want to knock off the table"

JANUARY

Wuthering Hodge

Hodge looked around to be sure no one was in the north room of the bookstore, and then continued his perusal of a paperback copy of *Wuthering Heights,* reasoning that he could always pretend to be playing with it or shredding the pages if anyone interrupted him.

Halfway through the chapter, he said to himself, "That's it! That's exactly what I've been wanting to say ever since we got to Thursday without the Boss Man putting out the notice for this month's Second Fridays reception. I want to cadge a few potato chips and sneak out the door while people are coming and going. And there's a particular paperweight in the gallery next door that I want to try to knock off the table this time. He just isn't paying attention!" With that, Hodge strolled into the reception area, flicked his tail in Keith's innocent and uncomprehending direction, and announced to a customer:

"'What is that apathetic being doing? Has he fallen into a lethargy, or is he dead?'"

"Nice kitty," said the customer, reaching down to pat Hodge on the head. "Damn," grumbled Hodge, "he didn't notice the double quotation marks or that cool double gerund."

FEBRUARY

Fine Dining

"You remembered the potato chips," said Hodge approvingly as Keith opened a bag and dumped the chips into a big bowl for the Second Fridays reception.

"Get your paws out of there!" said Keith. "Processed food isn't good for cats. Anyway, you're supposed to be an obligatory carnivore. From an evolutionary standpoint, you were meant to be eating rodents." Hodge stared at Keith, then strode purposefully over to the computer and began banging away at the keyboard, then indicated the screen with a flick of his tail. Keith peered across the desk and read:

The Bossman's Lunch
(to the tune of "Jamaica Farewell")

I was perched at a café table
Waiting patiently for my food.
I'd been there for about an hour;
This exercise had not improved my mood.
I waved frantically at my waiter
As he juggled a tray or three;

I yelled, "Mac, where's my quail in aspic?"
And he swanned over and said pleasantly:
"You were meant to be eating rodents,
Running dog of the bourgeoisie!
—Should be foraging through the trashcans!
Now shut your yap and don't bother me."

As Hodge pointedly turned his back on Keith a customer came through the door and asked, "Do you have *Thoughts of Chairman Mao*?"

"We all do from time to time," volunteered Hodge, helping himself to a potato chip.

"Nice kitty," said the customer.

MARCH

Roll Over, Blake

"Look at this cover illustration!" said a British customer as he handed Keith a paperback copy of William Blake's *Book of Urizen* and a $10 bill to pay for it. "Blake was ahead of his time in everything."

Hodge ambled over to investigate, hopping up on the computer table. "Nice draftsmanship," he opined.

"One of the good things about being on holiday is that you have a chance to get away from the political nutters in your country," said the customer.

"We have our own," Hodge pointed out, clambering up onto the customer's shoulder.

"What a handsome moggy," said the customer, somewhat taken aback, but too polite to object. Hodge looked at him with weary indulgence.

"I just heard on public radio today that the British National Party are trying to adopt 'Jerusalem' as their theme song," continued the customer. "Fortunately almost no one takes them seriously."

Thanking Keith for the book, he slipped past Hodge out the door. Keith reached out to grab Hodge in case the latter tried to escape,

"What a handsome moggy," said the customer.

but Hodge was already on his way over to the computer keyboard, looking fierce.

"What is it now?" asked Keith.

"Someone needs to write new words to it that no xenophobic fringe political party can get a pawhold on," Hodge told him, punching in a YouTube video of the King's College Choir performing "Jerusalem" with a church organ pulsing in the background. Then he began to type:

And did those feet,
Those furry feet,
Walk on the bookstore's floorboards brown?
And did those whiskers stark and sweet
Efface the humans' chronic frown?
And did a cat amuse himself?
And did he keep us all amused?
And was our spacious urban flat
With feline presence thus suffused?
Bring me my kibble and my bowl.
Bring my capacious litter box.
Bring me my scratching post of coir.
Bring me a plate of Nova lox!
Please understand: I am in charge.
Though at nine pounds I am not large,
I am the CAT, and that's the point:
A cat will always rule the joint.

With that, he sat back and raised his paw with the toes clenched, then opened the paw and raked downwards through the air.

"What the...?" demanded Keith.

"It's a variant on the trade unionist salute," explained Hodge. "It means Cat Power. Not the musician, of course—more like Cat World Domination. Get back to work, you."

"Please understand: I am in charge."

APRIL

The Cult of Chaos

"Boss Man, I've been thinking and I'd like to change my name," said Hodge to Keith as the latter unlocked the door to the bookstore on an early spring morning and began peeling off his gloves and coat.

"I'll feed you in a minute," said Keith. Hodge waited with exaggerated patience while Keith booted up the store's computer and put out fresh cat food and water. Preemptively positioning himself in front of the keyboard, Hodge logged on (having correctly intuited that the password would be his own name) and began typing.

"What's wrong with your name?" demanded Keith.

"It sounds stodgy," complained Hodge. "It even rhymes with stodgy. Some customers think it's supposed to be 'Haj,' and I like that, but it doesn't address the root problem."

"But you were named after Samuel Johnson's famous cat!" protested Keith.

"That just proves my point!" typed Hodge irritably. "What a pedestrian, Anglo-Saxon name. And anyway, it's a little off color, if you get my meaning. 'Johnson,' 'tommy,' 'john thomas'...I wonder if Samuel Johnson thought of it as his johnson when he was in the bog of the Ye Olde Cheshire Cheese dive bar getting rid of all the pints of ale he'd drunk?"

"It's not a dive bar, it's a venerable pub," complained Keith.

"In the eighteenth century it was a dive bar," replied Hodge. "And furthermore, what kind of people patronize an establishment with 'Cheese' in the title? Tourists and overly indulgent parents—the Cheesecake Factory. Chuck E. Cheese. You get my drift?"

"This is ridiculous," said Keith, "not to mention howlingly elitist. May I ask what you want to change your name to?"

"Chaos," typed Hodge promptly.

"That would suit you," said Keith grimly. "And what historical figure would you prefer to be associated with than Samuel Johnson?"

"Serge Gainsbourg?" hazarded Hodge.

The door opened before Keith could fully take this in, and an ethereal-looking young woman entered and said, "Good morning. Do you happen to have the sheet music to 'Fuir Le Bonheur De Peur Qu'il Ne Se Sauve' by Serge Gainsbourg—the Jane Birkin version from the 1980s?"

"I love that song!" shouted Hodge.

"What a nice kitty," said the customer, scratching him behind his ears. "A little loud, though."

"Actually I do, right here," said Keith, wondering how the music had ended up on the desk, and then looking suspiciously at Hodge, who placed a protective paw on the score for a moment, then looked up at the customer, began to purr, and removed the paw.

"If I want to memorize it I can use an online version," miaowed Hodge, "and you remind me of the incomparable Jane Birkin, doll. You're two of the best-looking broads I've ever seen. You both look like cats. She even sounds like a cat. Do you?"

"He's usually rather quiet," said Keith, packaging the music and handing it to the customer, who thanked him. "I don't know what's gotten into him today."

"'Chaos,'" replied Hodge. "To be continued. I'm not done yet."

. . . .

Keith returned from arranging sheet music on the big table across from the front door to find Hodge at the keyboard again, activating a YouTube recording of Marvin Gaye singing "Can I Get a Witness."

"I approve," he told the cat. "At least your musical tastes haven't gone completely south since you decided to pretend your name was Chaos."

Hodge snorted and continued typing with his nose and paws. Keith read over the cat's shoulder:

Can I get a whisker?
Can I get a paw?
Can I get a headbutt
To the upper jaw?

Then we'll feed the Chaos,
Then we'll fill his bowl,
Which will make him mellow
Down into his soul.

And may I remind you
That we do not bite.
We are close companions;
I don't want a fight.
(Repeat first verse)

"Hodge," said Keith. "How you manage to parody Marvin Gaye AND Van Morrison in three short verses is beyond me, but what worries me more is that this 'Chaos' persona you're flirting with sounds so bossy and self-absorbed. Look online and see how I described you to the interviewer for that article in the *Chicago Journal* a while back. Does that sound like this 'Chaos' cat?" He picked up a box of books and headed around the corner into the southeast alcove to shelve the contents.

Hodge looked affronted, then thoughtful, then intensely interested. Typing in "Hodge" and "Selected Works" and "Chicago Journal," he found the article and clicked on it. Skimming quickly till he got to his name, he read, "The cat, Hodge, whose previous home was the city pound, has since become a favorite with customers. 'Just a fearless, really smart, beautiful cat,' Peterson said."

"Chaos is all of those things!" protested Hodge, miaowing. Keith came back into the room and read the screen as Hodge continued typing:

"Sometimes I think you don't understand me at all. Maybe I'm not even your biological cat. Maybe I was adopted!"

"Hodge...," said Keith, at a temporary loss for words. "See where in the article it says 'city pound'?"

"I knew I came from the pound, but I still thought...I don't know..." Hodge looked briefly lost, miaowed plaintively, then leaped onto a high bookshelf, his face suddenly impassive, and slipped out of sight.

The clock struck 8. Keith turned off the lights and locked the door behind him, then pressed the button for the elevator, since he was hand-delivering a pair of first editions to one of the artists on the 10th floor. The bell rang somewhere in the depths of the building; a few minutes later the elevator arrived, and the friendly but taciturn elevator operator opened the door and nodded his greetings. As the elevator climbed slowly upward, each floor disappearing below through the glass doors, Keith asked the operator, "Did you ever live with someone for years and realize there was some huge misunderstanding?"

"Everything OK at home?" asked the operator, looking concerned.

"What?—sure, everything's fine!" said Keith. "I was just thinking about my cat."

The operator raised his eyebrows as the elevator arrived at the tenth floor. "Good night," said Keith abstractedly, exiting. The operator peered after him for a moment before shrugging his shoulders, closing the door, and beginning his descent.

• •

"You're open late," said a customer, pleased to find the bookstore open at 9 p.m. when it normally closed at 8 on weekdays except for Second Fridays.

"We're having a picnic," miaowed Hodge, through a mouthful of take-out fish sandwich from Miller's Pub. He was sitting on the desk close to Keith, with a paw in the tartar sauce, which Keith was pointedly ignoring.

"My cat Hodge and I decided to split a sandwich before I hit the

Hodge looked at him wearily and climbed into Keith's lap.

road," explained Keith. "I was out picking it up, but now we're open for a little while longer. Feel free to look around."

"Who is this lucky cat?" asked the customer rhetorically, politely concealing his astonishment, and reaching over to scratch Hodge behind his ears.

"I hope you don't do that at formal dinner gatherings," miaowed Hodge. "It's almost as bad as throwing salad plates—like in that classic cartoon series by James Thurber. To answer your question, I'm Hodge. I'm Keith's cat. I live here. All of which would have been clear to you if you'd done some elementary research on the internet. Everyone knows me. Have you been living under a rock?"

"Nice kitty," said the customer. Hodge looked at him wearily and climbed into Keith's lap, where he finished the rest of the sandwich, began to purr, and was soon deeply asleep. Keith lifted Hodge carefully into his cat bed, accepted $300 from the customer for an assortment of art books, turned off the light, and headed home to dinner.

MAY

Virginia Woolf Tribute Band Time

Hodge said that he would bite the customer himself.

For Keith had his work cut out for him. He had to tidy the place and put out the wine and potato chips for Second Fridays. The door would be opening all evening; shoppers were coming, each entrance a chance for Hodge to escape and force Keith to run after him. And then, thought Hodge, what a customer—fresh as if his mama hadn't taught him no manners; demanding that Keith slash $100 off the price of a first edition of *Mrs Dalloway*.

What a lark! What a plunge! What a tasty ankle.

The ensuing silence was broken by a sudden noise of ripping tweed and flesh.

JUNE

A Snitz in Time

The customer at the Second Fridays reception at Selected Works was tall, and broad enough that he nearly filled the doorway between the front of the store and the music room, making it difficult for others to squeeze by him. Keith poured the man a glass of wine and offered him potato chips. The customer accepted the offerings and announced loudly, "I haven't been to the South Side in ages. My wife dragged me here. I'm beat. I spent the whole day trapping the feral cats and kittens in our neighborhood and taking them to a better place." He grinned archly.

"You took them to be neutered and released?" asked Keith.

"No, I took them to Animal Control and told them to kill them," the man said cheerfully. Keith flushed, turned pale, and gripped the edge of his desk. As other customers in the store eyed the man with loathing, the ensuing silence was broken by a sudden noise of ripping tweed and flesh. The man staggered and bellowed and stepped toward the desk, exposing a half-naked backside and thighs and a grievously torn pair of trousers.

"I'm afraid I don't have a first aid kit or a needle and thread," said Keith. "There's a drugstore down the street on Wabash that should be able to help you."

"I could sue you for this," yelled the customer.

"I'm a senior partner at Kirkland and Ellis, and you can't sue a man because you split your trousers on his premises," protested an elegant woman holding a biography of Swinburne.

The man muttered something, dropped his wineglass on the floor, breaking it and spilling the contents, and ran out the door, awkwardly attempting to clutch the remains of his pants together. It was a warm night and not coat weather.

"What a creep," said the lawyer. "I felt like leaving the room the minute I got near him."

Keith handed around more wine, wishing he had something even stronger, and the outraged customers, who had been muttering to each other in tones of satisfied vicarious vengeance, gradually subsided and paid for their purchases. After they had gone, Hodge emerged from behind a shelf of books in the music room and hopped onto the desk, purring. Keith detached a thread of tweed from his whiskers. "This rates a fish sandwich from Miller's Pub," he told Hodge.

Hodge purred more loudly and head-butted Keith's hand, then walked over to the computer keyboard and typed, "It's called a snitz across the tuchus. Jewish antifascists used it on their enemies in the late 1940s in London. You can look it up."

JULY

Playing Our Song

Keith returned from buying cat food and opened the door of the bookstore to the unfamiliar sound of spoken poetry. "Your man appears to be having some kind of out-of-body experience," reported Hodge, looking up from a video of the Rolling Stones' memorial concert for Brian Jones in London in 1969.

Keith peered at the screen, where Mick Jagger was addressing several hundred thousand people on a summer day in Hyde Park, reading aloud from Shelley's Adonais,

> *"The One remains, the many change and pass;*
> *Heaven's light forever shines, Earth's shadows fly;*
> *Life, like a dome of many-coloured glass,*
> *Stains the white radiance of Eternity,*
> *Until Death tramples it to fragments.—"*

"What is he going on about?" typed Hodge irritably. "I'm waiting to hear 'Jumping Jack Flash,' because it's my theme song."

"That song suits you," admitted Keith, "at least, the name does, but why do you identify with it?"

"You don't know what I went through as a kitten before I got to the pound," retorted Hodge, still typing. "If you did, you'd be feeding me fish sandwiches daily just to make me feel better."

"Why do I sense a ploy here?" Keith mused aloud, raising his voice slightly to be heard over Shelley.

Hodge stared at him for a moment, his tail puffing up and his ears going back. Then, as the band began to play, he typed:

"The One remains, the many change and pass;
And I invite them all to kiss my ass."

AUGUST

Advice

"You won't be seeing me for a while," Jeff McNary, a friend of the bookstore, told Keith and Hodge. "I'm going back to Cambridge. I've been accepted into the writing program at Harvard."

"Those East Coast intellectual types will eat you alive," miaowed Hodge.

"What's the matter with you now?" demanded Jeff. Hodge had hoped that McNary's cosmopolitanism would enable him to understand spoken cat, but now realized it was not happening. He hopped onto the desk and typed what he had miaowed.

McNary read what was on the screen, peered down at Hodge and raised one eyebrow. "'Eat me alive'—yeah, like that time you tried?"

"Oh, don't exaggerate," typed Hodge, staring intently at McNary over his shoulder and touch-typing with his paws. "What's this great American novel you're going to write supposed to be about?"

"Don't look at me like that—it ain't gonna be about no cat," McNary replied.

"Why will people not learn from the mistakes of others?" typed

"THEY WEREN'T ABOUT CATS."

Hodge, returning his gaze to the keyboard. "Do you have any idea how many people devote their lives to writing books they can't get published, or that never sell more than a few hundred copies and end up remaindered and eventually pulped? And why?"

"I don't know—insipid characters, improbable story lines, failure of imagination?" suggested Jeff, shifting his position slightly, and regarding Hodge's behind warily.

"NO," typed Hodge. "How on earth did YOU get into Harvard? The answer is obvious: THEY WEREN'T ABOUT CATS."

SEPTEMBER

The Labors of Hodge

Hodge emerged from his carrier feeling a little disoriented from the ride on the Number 6 bus, but happy to be back at Keith's apartment for a visit.

"Ma'at!" he cried joyfully as the resident cat rounded a corner and came face to face with him. "Who loves ya, baby?"

"What's HE doing here?" Ma'at howled at Keith, dismayed.

"He's just home for Labor Day. The building is closed tomorrow for the holiday, so the store is taking a day off," announced Keith.

"Oh, crumbs!" exploded Ma'at, hopping clumsily up onto the dining-room table and looking disgustedly down at Hodge, who followed her in a graceful, arcing leap.

"Ma'at," he said, "I've written a poem for you."

"A what?"

"Words to express my affection. I stole the tune from Mott the Hoople. I would never have gotten into that band except for you. I was looking up your name online and I was too young to know how to spell it. Check this out." After bashing away with his paws and nose at the keyboard of a laptop that was parked on the table pumping out vintage Thomas Mapfumo, he managed to stop the African music, with a muttered "Sorry about that, Lion of Zimbabwe," and start a YouTube recording of "All the Young Dudes." He began to type.

"What IS this 'music'?" demanded Ma'at, querulously.

"Keith, what on earth are you playing that for?" echoed Keith's wife, Gail, emerging from the kitchen with her arms covered in flour up to the elbows. "I can't cook to that adolescent caterwauling. Turn it off or I'm going on strike."

"Hang on a minute, ladies," said Hodge. "Ian Hunter isn't to everyone's taste, but I love him, and Ma'at deserves an anthem and I'm writing new and better lyrics right now." Gail, Keith, and Ma'at peered down at him as he banged out the following:

The Ballad of Ma'at the Ca'at with Apologies to Mott the Hoople

Well Ma'at the Ca'at she knows where it's at
In a box or bag that kitty ain't no slag
She can accelerate to 30 mph in the hallway
And Hodge steals food from people's plates
And Bamba of blessed memory could sure express himself with pee
(He said it was pure poetry)
Elevator man is crazy, says Obama will betray us
You can't expect a POTUS to obey us

All the young dudes
Furry the news
Whiskerface dudes
Furry the news
All the young dudes (I want to hear you)
Furry the news (I want to see you)
Whiskerface dudes (and I want to talk to you all of you)
Furry the news

Now Ma'at looks sweet and she ought to be a queen
Snakes in Egypt called her part of a real mean team
But she can love oh yes she can love

Yeah our cat at home chases beetles under stones
Ma'at never got off on that cat-toy stuff
She likes her prey alive and kicking
Now I've drunk a lot of wine and I'm feeling fine
Got to race some cat to bed
Oh is there cat fur all around
Or is he sitting on my head?

Winded by his exertions, Hodge sat back and displayed the screen.

"What's this about 'racing some cat to bed'?" asked Ma'at suspiciously. "You're supposed to sleep in the broom closet."

"That was actually original—David Bowie wrote it, I didn't," said Hodge. "I just thought it was a nice objective for a human to have, so I didn't mess with that part. Anyway, what's with the cold welcome, baby? I feel like Heathcliff on his first night at Wuthering Heights, plucked from the gutter in Liverpool only to be kicked out of bed in Yorkshire and forced to sleep on the landing."

"I've seen Heathcliff in the comics and you don't look anything like him," reported Ma'at.

"That's the nicest thing you've said to me since I arrived, you uncultivated little hellion," responded Hodge, indulgently.

"Next time," miaowed Ma'at, looking longingly at Keith, "couldn't you just put out a big bowl of kibble and a quart of water and leave him alone in the store?"

• • • • • • • • • • • • • • • • • • • •

"Hey," announced Ma'at to Hodge, "it isn't true what you wrote about me in that weird song you were playing yesterday." The two of them were sitting at opposite ends of the living room on Labor Day as Ma'at sought to keep as much distance between them as possible, and Hodge simply sought to practice good cat manners in another cat's home. Surprised and pleased that Ma'at was speaking to him at all, Hodge answered mildly, "But I've seen you accelerate to 30 mph in the hallway! That's one of the reasons the humans think you have Egyptian Mau blood. You're like a little cheetah."

"Not that part!" said Ma'at irritably, and then, in tones of rising indignation, "You said I eat bugs. You said I don't like cat toys. It isn't true. I've never eaten a bug in my life. I'm scared of bugs."

"I'm sorry I called you out of your name like that," said Hodge. "I thought you were a mighty huntress, the Diana of our chambers, but it's true that I never actually saw you with live prey in your mouth. What kind of cat toys do you like? I have several that the customers brought me. I like them, but if it will make you happy I can smuggle some home with me next time I come back here for a holiday."

The prospect of Hodge returning to the apartment with or without toys was one that Ma'at clearly found depressing. "I like all kinds of cat toys," she said dolefully, "but the only one I really love is lost. I haven't seen it in years."

"What was it?" asked Hodge.

"It actually had a name. You can look it up online. It was called Great Balls of Fur. It was a silly name but it was the best toy ever. Oh, I miss it so!"

"Can you describe it?" asked Hodge. "How did you come by it?"

Ma'at looked at him thoughtfully for a moment, and then said, "Come with me and I'll tell you about it." She jumped off the coffee table, knocking over an empty martini glass ("Bother!"), and sprinted down the hallway into the dining room, where she jumped up on the table and knocked over a stack of books, causing a chain reaction that ended with an African violet tumbling onto the floor amidst a hail of dirt and broken terra cotta. Hodge followed her, landing neatly at the other end of the table without touching anything. "It stands to reason that we're going to knock stuff over if they keep it lying around," he said gallantly. "I'm always knocking books off the shelf at the store," he lied.

Ma'at ignored him and stalked over to a computer on the table, where to Hodge's amazement she began to type with her nose and paws, keying in a YouTube address and choosing a vintage recording by Jerry Lee Lewis. Then she began typing what looked to Hodge like lines of verse.

"I thought I was the only cat that knew how to do that," said Hodge.

"You think you're so smart," said Ma'at, pausing to stare insolently at him. "I'm not 'uncultivated' like you said. And I have more street sense than you. I was living on the street when I found these humans. I was only a kitten and I was almost starving, and pregnant. I've been pregnant and I've been spayed. Spayed is better."

Feeling a bit overwhelmed, Hodge said weakly, "Well, the Boss Man got me from Animal Control. I could have been killed."

"No way. I've heard the humans say that you were such an adorable kitten that you probably spent all of 45 minutes at Animal Control before Keith came by there looking for a bookstore cat and snapped you up. I had to cross two lanes of moving traffic to follow my humans back here."

"Thank you for passing on that compliment," said Hodge. "But you were going to tell me about this missing toy?"

"Right," said Ma'at. "Here is what happened. And unlike you, I'm telling the truth and not embroidering it with stuff to make myself look like Diane Chambers or whoever you were talking about a minute ago."

Peering over Ma'at's shoulder as she typed, Hodge read:

My auntie showed up with a fancy white sack
It had red sequins and designs on the back
She reached in there—I wouldn't dare—
Goodness gracious Great Balls of Fur
She pulled this object out like I'd never seen
A furry yellow ball with legs pink and green
Gave it to me, oh what a spree
Goodness gracious Great Balls of Fur

I sorta kiss it first, woo...it feels good
And then I pounce on it, to learn to hold it like a birder should
It's fine, all mine
I wanna tell you it's di-vi-i-i-ine

I treat it like I was Attila the Hun
It may be nervous but I'm having fun
It flew away, came back next day
Goodness gracious Great Balls of Fur

I sometimes hide it just to give it a rest—
Like, once I sneaked it in the purse of a guest
(I like to pack;
She brought it back,

Thank goodness)—
Gracious! Great Balls of Fur

I say goodness gracious Great Balls of Fur
I shake its nerves and I rattle its brain
Too much excitement drives a kitty insane
I broke its will, oh what a thrill
Goodness gracious Great Balls of Fur

"It sounds like quite a toy," said Hodge. "Maybe I can help you find it. Clearly you need it back."

"But I've looked EVERYWHERE for it!" wailed Ma'at.

"I can bring a fresh eye to the problem," pointed out Hodge. "I don't live here. In fact I'm going to start right now, and I'm not going to stop till I can put it back in your pretty little paw. Neither rain nor snow nor dark of night will keep this servant from the swift completion of his appointed rounds! After all, you're supposed to be my girlfriend."

"It's a sunny Labor Day weekend," said Ma'at, ungratefully. But Hodge didn't hear her. He was already in the kitchen, starting his systematic search.

....

Seven hours later, Hodge was back in the kitchen again and covered in dust. He knew more than he wanted to about his hosts, their taste in music and literature, and their priorities, of which a scrupulous attention to cleanliness and order was less salient than their being persons of what an author he liked had once described as "broad humane culture." He was tired and dispirited, but his eyes widened when a small, brown mouse emerged from a cabinet and begin wandering toward him, apparently so lost in thought that it didn't see him until it was only a few inches away.

"Ack!" cried the mouse—"Guest Cat is out of kibble units! Here you are, Mr. Gray Cat, sir," as it hopped onto a bag of cat food and began tearing open the side of it with its teeth, so that the kibble spilled on the floor.

"Well, I am kind of hungry," Hodge admitted.

"Yes, sir, the mouse is aware of that and is pleased to be fulfilling a socially useful function," replied the mouse, scurrying back several feet.

"Don't worry," Hodge assured him. "Mice are not my dish of tea. And thank you for the kibble. I'll get back to it shortly but now I'm on a quest."

"A quest for something better than kibble?" said the mouse. "I can open anything you like as long as it doesn't require an opener of cans. Wait, as you were—I mean, a can opener. Perhaps you would like some tasty organic butter of peanuts? Or are you thirsty? I know how to turn on the kitchen faucet. I could get you some good nourishing dihydrogen monoxide. Or I know where there's an open bottle of Châteauneuf-du-Pape AOC. The human units put it out so it could breathe for a while before they drink it with dinner. Those humans are smart. They didn't go to college for nothing."

"Thanks, but cats don't drink wine, and there's enough water in my dish," replied Hodge. "Actually, you look like you know your way around here."

"Affirmative," replied the mouse. "I know everything. Thanks a petabyte for recognizing that."

"Maybe you could help me find something?" asked Hodge.

"6.62606957 × 10-34 m2 kg / s," replied the mouse immediately.

"What?" asked Hodge, now thoroughly bewildered.

"Planck's constant," explained the mouse. "Wasn't that what you were looking for?"

"I'm looking for a cat toy," said Hodge. "And please don't look like you're going to run away—I don't mean I propose to use you as one."

"Thank you, thank you, Your Supreme Excellency. Thank you ten to the sixth power," replied the mouse, clearly relieved.

"Have you seen a cat toy that consists of a yellow fur ball with pink and green legs?" asked Hodge.

"Only when I go off my meds," replied the mouse. "I'm joking—little funny there," it added, seeing Hodge's disappointment. "Actually I think I know where it is."

"You do?" exclaimed Hodge.

"My wife stole it," said the mouse. Hodge stared in astonishment, not least because this was the first simple declarative statement he had heard the mouse make.

Hodge backed off to avoid alarming the mouse, which appeared a moment later at the entrance to its mouse hole carrying a rather dirty and rumpled cat toy.

"I can talk like other people," said the mouse defensively. "At work, for instance, I speak standard business English."

"Where do you work?" asked Hodge.

"I work in a rat's office. He's a venture capitalist. We're off for Labor Day," explained the mouse. "But we seem to be digressing from the subject, from our most important subject. If you'll pardon me for a moment I'll retrieve your cat toy for you. Don't go away. You're doing an excellent job of not going away. And please refrain from committing suicide."

"Why would I ever...oh, never mind," said Hodge.

The mouse darted into a small hole in the kitchen wall that Hodge had somehow overlooked. Hodge put his ear to the hole and could hear it rummaging around.

"Where's the toy?" demanded the mouse, apparently to itself. "Did some fascist scuzzball try to clean the place and hide it? Every time they clean up this mouse hole I can't find anything for a week. They claim they're helping. The British said they were helping when they colonized India. Oh, there it is. Good, we can return it to his Supreme Cathood. I like Mr. Gray Cat. He's my new favorite person."

Hodge backed off to avoid alarming the mouse, which appeared a moment later at the entrance to its mouse hole carrying a rather dirty and rumpled cat toy matching the description from Ma'at. "Here you go," it said, offering the toy to him. "Bon voyage, Creature from the Blue Planet. I need to go get started making the chow units. We're having some feral gerbils over. They're making me cook a vegetarian dish and I need extra time to study the recipe. Remember the Maine. Forget the Alamo." Hodge took the toy in his mouth and then dropped it to say thank you, but the mouse had already vanished.

....

"You didn't have to tear open the cat food! They'll feed you if you ask nicely," said Ma'at, poking disgustedly at the bag of kibble that the mouse had torn open for Hodge. "I can tell you don't live in a house with people." Hodge looked sad for a moment, because the domestic environment, almost always a treat, had grown on him, even though he had spent the day getting dusty and frustrated looking for Ma'at's toy—which he had now hidden behind the cat food bag while trying to think of a properly impressive way to return it to her.

"That wasn't me," he said. "It was a mouse."

"Did you kill him?" demanded Ma'at.

"Of course not. He was a gentleman," said Hodge, obscurely.

"HE WAS A MOUSE," said Ma'at.

"A gentleman and a mouse," said Hodge, reaching behind the cat food and pulling out Ma'at's long-lost toy. "Ma'at, I believe you were missing this?"

Ma'at stared. She approached the toy carefully and sniffed it. Then she grinned ecstatically and tossed it up in the air, grabbed it on its way down, and flopped over on the kitchen floor rabbit-kicking it with her back feet.

"Ooh, you found it! You're my hero," she said.

"In that case," said Hodge, "would you consider showing me some love? I mean, you're supposed to be my girlfriend—yow!" He broke off as Ma'at jumped on his tail.

"I love you!" she howled. "You found my toy. I love you forever!"

"Couldn't you find a more genteel way of express—hey!" Ma'at had wrapped her paws around his middle in her exuberance and was mauling him the way she had been mauling her toy.

"Whee!" said Ma'at. "I have it back. Hodge found my cat toy. I'll never let him go now." She loosened her hold for a moment. Hodge bolted and hid in his carrier in a closet.

• •

Hodge rose at dawn, looking forward to another day of helping Keith sell books and sheet music at Selected Works. He proceeded cautiously down the hall to score some kibble. He had missed dinner because he was hiding from Ma'at, and was ravenous. After a substantial meal—the contents of his bowl, augmented by something from the bag the mouse had raked open—he jumped up onto the dining room table and stared out at the pretty old 1920s buildings on Everett Avenue glowing rosily in the reflected light from the sun rising over the lake. "Be careful what you ask for," he warned the sleeping residents of East Hyde Park.

OCTOBER

Ma'at's Midnight Confession

Keith, home for the evening, was about to check the next day's weather on the home computer when he looked more closely at the screen and found that it read:

For Hodge, Who Found My Favorite Cat Toy and Made Me Happy Again

(To the tune of Chant, by Little Peggy Mauch)

I will follow him,
Ever since I saw his whiskered face,
There isn't a cat box too deep,
Nor closed bedroom door that can keep,
Keep me away, away from his tail.

I love him, I love him, I love him,
Especially his tail,
Which I like to jump on.

He'll always be my focus, my object, my compass,
Especially that tail, that tail, that tail.

I will follow him,
Follow him wherever he may hide,
I'll watch and I'll wait by the door,
And sooner or later you know
I'll pounce on his tail.
(That beautiful tail.)

We will follow him,
Follow him wherever he may go,
There isn't a bathtub too deep,
Or shelving so high it can keep,
Keep us away, away from that tail.

There isn't a closet too deep,
A shoulder so high it can keep,
Keep me away, away from his tail.

"Gail," Keith called. "Have you been channeling Ma'at?"

"Not to my knowledge," said Gail, appearing in the kitchen doorway with a martini in each hand. She gave one to Keith, who said, "Look at this. I didn't write it and we haven't had guests recently."

Gail read the poem. She and Keith looked at each other.

"Could Hodge have taught her how to do that?" asked Keith.

"Maybe, but I'm more worried about the content," said Gail. "This amounts to stalking—or it will the next time she has an opportunity."

"We have till Thanksgiving to figure something out," said Keith. "That buys us a little time and we're going to need it."

"Of course I'm a stalker: I'm a CAT," announced Ma'at reproachfully, hopping up onto the table.

"Nice kitty," replied Keith automatically.

NOVEMBER

No Place Like Home for the Holidays

"I wish you were open on Thanksgiving," said a customer as he paid for his books. "I'd love to spend it in the front room reading and looking out the window at the lakefront and Grant Park. Instead I have to drive to the suburbs and try to make conversation with my mother's third husband's family."

"Thank you," said Keith. "We'll reopen as usual the day after Thanksgiving, and you're welcome to hang out here and recover."

Hodge, who had been lounging contentedly on the radiator looking at the pigeons, leaped to attention, his eyes wide and his tail puffing up.

"What is it now?" asked Keith as the door closed behind the customer.

"Are you going to make me go home with you on Thanksgiving when you know Ma'at wants to devour me?" demanded Hodge.

Hodge's miaowing rarely made any sense to Keith, who therefore moved aside obligingly when Hodge jumped up on the desk and, using his nose and paws, keyed in a YouTube recording of a very young Joan Baez singing a late medieval Scottish ballad called, confusingly, "The Great Silkie of Sule Skerry."

"Hodge," protested Keith immediately, "this music is lugubrious and the words are borderline incomprehensible. It's pretty but it has no soul. I don't care if it's survived for 500 years; it has no business in the store."

"Philistine!" typed Hodge. "It just needs the lyrics updated." He began to type, and Keith read:

A patient human tries to sleep,
Forgetting that he owns a cat,
And meanwhile in the other room
A beast arises from the mat.

And he came that night to his host's bed feet,
And a comely pest I'm sure was he,
Saying, "Here am I, your neglected cat,
Although deep in sleep you may be.

"I am a cat upon the bed,
And you're the human under me.
I'm stomping briskly up and down,
With claws extended, as you see."

And he had ta'en a silvery paw,
And he had placed it on Keith's knee,
Saying, "Don't you know a cat can starve
If you don't feed him hourly?

"It's true my bowl is full of food,
And you've topped up my water dish,
But when the clock says 4 a.m.,
One's thoughts will turn toward tuna fish."

And so it came to pass in that autumn dark:
Keith's day began while it was night.
He fed Hodge tuna from the can
Because he was too smart to fight.

"How," asked Keith, "would you like to spend Thanksgiving alone in the store with a big bowl of kibble?"

To his surprise, Hodge beamed at him and began to purr approvingly.

• •

"What IS that?" demanded Keith, returning from a short excursion to pick up cat food, to find an unfamiliar song resounding loudly through the bookstore.

"Joan Baez led me to Bob Dylan," miaowed Hodge—"not literally, but I like this old tune and I've written you some new lyrics that you'll be able to use soon, if you insist on bringing me home for Thanksgiving for Ma'at to ambush me and persecute me."

Keith saw that Hodge had activated a YouTube video of Billy Bragg covering "Lay Down Your Weary Tune," and that the cat had also typed something on the screen.

"Not exactly a mystical experience early in the morning at Big Sur or whatever inspired the original, but powerful in its own way, don't you think?" asked Hodge, menacingly. Keith read, aloud:

"Joan Baez led me to Bob Dylan."

Lie down, you furry cat, lie down,
And please stop biting me.
It's 4 a.m. and I'm still asleep,
Which is what you should be.
Go watch the world from the window sill.
Look out for mice and rats.
Patrol for possums and fat raccoons
And errant alley cats.
And please stop pouncing on my feet
As if you think they're mice.
I'm flesh and blood underneath the sheets,
This aggro is not nice.
Lie down, you bookstore cat, lie down.
Kindly stop pawing me.
It's 4 a.m. and we're all asleep,
Which is what you should be.
Ow! Stop that! Let go of my foot. Get out of here [fade]

"Hodge," said Keith, "you can threaten me all you want, but you're coming home for Thanksgiving. The store will be closed. In fact, we need to leave now—the time got away from me and I need to help Gail with the prep for tomorrow's dinner. Here's your cat carrier."

"No way!" yelped Hodge, who hadn't realized that it was already the eve of the dreaded holiday. He leaped seven feet in the air and landed on the highest shelf in the store, then peered down at Keith like a gargoyle. Keith suppressed a curse as the door opened and a customer walked in, saying, "Happy Thanksgiving. Do you happen to have *Turkey: A Modern History,* by Erik Zurcher?"

"Yes, I do," said Keith, and looked inside the book to find the price.

Up above him, Hodge froze, then began to purr, first quietly and then loudly. The customer looked up. "What a nice kitty!" he said, as Hodge rapidly descended the bookcase and hopped onto the desk. Hodge briefly head-butted the customer, then turned and slipped serenely into his cat carrier and settled himself on the small blanket inside it. "Ready to hit the road, chief," he miaowed to Keith.

Keith handed the book to the customer, took the proffered bill, and

"Ready to hit the road, chief," he miaowed to Keith.

gave him his change. The customer wished him and Hodge a good evening, and closed the door behind him on his way out into the hall.

On the way back to Keith's apartment on the crowded Number 6 bus, Hodge indulged in a rare surge of gratitude toward the last customer of the day. "If that guy hadn't mentioned turkey I wouldn't have remembered that it was part of Thanksgiving at the Boss Man's home—maybe not at all, or maybe not till I was sitting there all alone in the store with a dish of stone-cold kibble," he thought. "I owe him."

....

"Hodge! You're back!" exclaimed Ma'at as Hodge and Keith came through the front door. "What am I, chopped liver?" demanded Keith, as Ma'at, who normally adored him, failed to register his presence, and jumped onto the top of Hodge's cat carrier.

Hodge hunkered down into his blanket as Ma'at leaned over and tried to stick her paw into the carrier. "I came for the turkey, not for you," he grumbled, laying back his ears and puffing up his tail.

"Ma'at," said Keith, putting the carrier on the floor, "you need to leave Hodge alone. Give him his space. He's our guest."

Gail emerged from the kitchen carrying two martinis, gave one to Keith, looked down at Ma'at, and drank deeply from the other.

"Ma'at," she said. "Behave. You can talk to Hodge whenever you want to, but you are not to pounce on his tail, or chase him, or stalk him. And whatever you do, don't ambush him when he's using the cat box!" Keith picked Ma'at up and placed her amid the clutter on the dining room table, then let Hodge out of his carrier.

"But I love him!" squeaked Ma'at.

"I love turkey, but I don't plan to maul it tomorrow," retorted Hodge, keeping his distance and hopping up onto the sideboard. "I'll ask nicely and they'll give me some. And if you don't get a grip on yourself, you little maenad, you'll spend Thanksgiving Dinner locked in the bedroom, and I'll get your portion too. M'm." He began to purr.

....

The Thanksgiving turkey was perfuming the apartment, while Keith was brushing cat hair off his smoking jacket and Gail was absorbed in concocting complex cocktails with exotic home-grown ingredients. Ma'at and Hodge were more estranged than ever, after having briefly turned the bed into a battleground in which yowling, jumping, and claws had figured significantly and they had been summarily ejected. That had been just before 4 a.m., almost 12 hours earlier, but the passage of time had not improved either cat's mood. Nonetheless, after a brief nap, they found themselves flung together once again at the foot of the stove, both drawn inexorably to the smell of roasting turkey.

"You can forget that idea you had last night about getting my portion of turkey," Ma'at told Hodge. "I plan to ask for it nicely and eat it like a lady and not like a 'maenad,' whatever that is. And no one is locking me in the bedroom. I got locked out of it because of you—that's bad enough."

The Thanksgiving turkey was perfuming the apartment.

"Because of me? Who jumped on whom?"

"I jumped on you because you claimed I was snoring! I wasn't. I was hunting in my sleep and making hunting noises. Cats do that."

"I'm sure I don't," retorted Hodge. "And I'm delighted that you plan to approach your turkey with more delicacy than you bring to our relationship."

"You used to say I was your girlfriend," said Ma'at bitterly. "You found my favorite cat toy for me after I lost it. You wrote weird poetry about how I came from ancient Egypt. And now you just pick on me. What happened? What did I do wrong?"

"The moment you decided you liked me after giving me the cold shoulder and the silent treatment for months, you grabbed me and started rabbit-kicking me and said you were never going to let go of me," snarled Hodge. "I felt like Keith Richards being mobbed by rabid Rolling Stones fans back before they had good security. I thought you were going to kill me."

"I was just expressing affection!" howled Ma'at.

"Will you two take it somewhere else?" asked Gail, opening the oven door to check on the turkey.

"I'm getting out of here before the dame in the Chanel suit steps on my lovely and innocent tail," said Hodge to Ma'at. "Come with me and I'll explain something to you." Ma'at followed him out of the kitchen, but with a wistful backward glance at Gail and at the oven door.

The laptop was still on the dining room table, though it was now surrounded by a rather formal arrangement of linens, china and cutlery in preparation for Thanksgiving Dinner. Hodge jumped onto the table. Ma'at hopped clumsily after him, exercising special care and not knocking anything off it this time. The doorbell rang and Keith admitted a large group of guests and escorted them into the living room for drinks, where Gail joined them.

"Listen to this," said Hodge, using his nose and paws to key in a YouTube video of Roberta Flack singing "The First Time Ever I Saw Your Face."

"This is how a lady expresses affection," said Hodge. "You can tell that dame has class. She's not operating out of a mosh pit. In fact, move over and I'll show you how you should be talking to me." He began to bang out a set of lyrics on the computer keyboard. Ma'at listened to the music intently, with her eyes wide open. Hodge finished typing and waved her over to the screen with his tail. It read:

The first time I saw your furry face
I thought that you were part Siamese.
You were thin, dark and intelligent,
And as sinuous as a weasel—
Like a mustelid, if you please.

You are the best cat in the universe.
You are discreet, agile and bright.
You are sweet, loyal and curious,
And on top of all that, you bite, my love,
And on top of all that you bite.

"But the first time I saw your face I didn't think you were part Siamese. I just thought you were a jerk," said Ma'at. "And are you really rhyming 'Siamese' with 'weasel'?"

"Poetic license!" miaowed Hodge.

"You ARE kind of like a mustelid," admitted Ma'at. "I saw this nature show on TV with the humans once. It was all about wolverines."

"I was thinking more of a ferret or an ermine!" protested Hodge irritably.

"But I don't understand this part where I'm supposed to say you're the best cat in the universe, and that you're sweet and loyal," continued Ma'at.

"What's not to understand about that?" Hodge demanded.

"It just doesn't sound like you," replied Ma'at. "And what about me? Are you saying you're better than me?"

"Have you been reading second wave feminists?" asked Hodge.

"Where would I find anything like that around here?" deflected Ma'at, unsure what he was talking about and not at all interested in finding out. "Anyway, I do like the tune a lot. I want to try singing it. I like the way she bends the notes. I've never heard anyone do that."

"Knock yourself out, kid, but I don't know if you've got the pipes to do it justice," advised Hodge. "Roberta Flack is special."

Ma'at sat back and opened her mouth wide.

"The first time I saw your furry face

I thought that you were part SI-A-MEEEEEEEEEEEE-EEE-EEE-EEE-EEE-EEEEEEEEEEESE"—

"WHAT ARE YOU DOING TO HER?" yelled Keith and Gail almost in unison, racing from the living room and down the hall, followed by a posse of alarmed guests with their mouths half stuffed with elegant hors d'oeuvre, some clutching martini glasses and splashing their drinks on the floor.

Ma'at looked confused.

"It wasn't ME," smirked Hodge."

• •

The guests were sated with Thanksgiving turkey and ancillaries, and Gail and Keith were handing around coffee and post-prandial cocktails, when one of the guests asked plaintively, "Could we move to the living room? I've been sitting in this chair for two hours and my posterior ass-like unit is getting sore."

The guests rose, gathered up their cups and glasses, and filed out of the dining room and down the hall. Deep in the forest of plants in the west window, Hodge said to Ma'at, "You know that guy better than I do. Does he always talk like that?"

"His father worked at McDonnell-Douglas. Maybe he thinks he was assembled by structural engineers," said Ma'at.

"You know, kid, you look like a Rousseau in those plants," Hodge observed.

"What kind of bird is that?" demanded Ma'at suspiciously.

"Never mind," sighed Hodge.

"I wonder if this would be a good time to ask them nicely for some turkey?" asked Ma'at. "Do you think they'll understand us now that they're away from the table? Or will they just think we want to play or something? I didn't want to bother them when they were eating."

"'Bother' them'?" snorted Hodge. "The trick is to not let them notice you when you stick your paw up on their plate and bring the turkey on down to your level."

"I didn't see you doing that," pointed out Ma'at.

"The opportunity did not present itself," said Hodge sententiously. "They were all too damned intent on their food. And worse yet, everyone was getting along! The best time to pull that stunt is when people are arguing with each other and gesticulating and looking anywhere but down at the table."

"Did we miss our chance?" asked Ma'at, suddenly wistful.

"Don't look so tragic," said Hodge. "This is our moment! They're way down at the other end of the apartment. The turkey is on the kitchen counter. There's plenty for both of us. Let's go." He slithered out from beneath the overhanging fronds of something and hopped onto the floor.

"You don't mean—we jump up on the counter and ...?" said Ma'at, cowering behind a large fern and looking appalled.

"Well, that's MY plan," said Hodge. "You just have to listen, and make sure you jump down and look innocent when you hear them coming. They aren't going to check your whiskers."

Ma'at sniffed deeply. Her expression changed, becoming rapt and vacant. She followed Hodge into the kitchen, and the two of them jumped up onto the counter and began gnawing away at the copious remains of a very large turkey.

Half an hour later, the cats were back in the plants in a tryptophan haze, gently polishing the bones of a big turkey leg that Hodge had had the forethought to grab in his teeth and abscond with, in case, as he put it, "We go into a turkey coma and stop paying attention and get caught." Too full and too sleepy to start fighting, they drifted into a deep sleep.

Around 9 p.m. Keith and Gail managed to get their guests to leave, by elaborate references to all the work they had to do in the morning. Putting things back in the fridge, Keith said, "We sure made inroads on that turkey."

"The carving looks pretty raggedy-assed, but I guess no one noticed," said Gail, casually inspecting the carcass.

....

Hodge was still under the influence of the quarter of a turkey he had consumed on Thanksgiving while his owners were out of the room, when Keith bundled him unceremoniously into his cat carrier on Friday

"You don't mean—we jump up on the counter and ...?"

morning to return to the bookstore.

"This carrier seems heavier than it did on the way home," Keith observed to Gail. "Has he been gorging on kibble?"

"I do not propose to dignify that question by responding to it," interrupted Hodge. "Some people are so desperate for conviviality that they'll eat anything as long as someone else is in the room. I am not one of them. They tend to hang out in suburban chain restaurants. Nap time. Check in with you at the office."

Traffic in Chicago was surprisingly light that morning, and the Number 6 bus reached Van Buren Street 20 minutes after Keith and Hodge had boarded it. Hodge awoke feeling serene and refreshed, and yawned elaborately.

"What a nice kitty!" said the student who had been sitting next to them.

Hodge shuddered and retreated deeper into his carrier.

DECEMBER

Noel

"I see we're back in the Middle Ages, but at least this one has some rhythm," said Keith approvingly after Hodge had used his paws and nose to key in a YouTube video of the Hiram Madrigals singing Patapan, the Burgundian Christmas carol.

"Actually the 17th century," maiowed Hodge, and began typing something on the computer screen.

"It's almost Christmas and I'm not in the mood for any literary aggro from you," warned Keith as Hodge finished typing and gestured toward the screen with his tail.

Hodge walked over to Keith and head-butted him affectionately, and began to purr.

"You've BEEN fed," Keith protested, and then adjusted his glasses and read:

Cat and man are now as one.
Man and cat have lots of fun.

"Merry Christmas, Boss Man!" added Hodge.

Queen Babushka
BL

JANUARY

The Island Full of Fish

ON THE ROAD TO MANDALAY

"Haven't you forgotten something?" asked Hodge by way of welcome, as Keith pulled off his coat, opened his backpack, and began settling in for another day of work at the bookstore.

"FISH SANDWICH," added Hodge, loudly, when Keith failed to register the question.

Keith booted up his computer, and Hodge dove in between Keith's hands and began typing on the keyboard with his nose and paws, wearily recalling that a complex philosophical question he had asked aloud while home with Keith and Gail for the Christmas holiday had been met with the observation, "Now he's mouthing off about something in the kitchen."

Keith, reading the query, said, "Fish sandwiches are for special occasions. Like when you realized your name was Hodge and that you're my cat and you belong here, after you were worrying about not being our 'biological cat.' That, and every now and then you can probably expect one as tribute from that young barfly who credits you with turning his love life around. They are not going to be on the menu every day, so deal with it."

Hodge retreated, more affronted than disappointed, and the door opened. The customer who walked in looked fearfully around the room and asked Keith in a low voice, "Do you have the collected poems of Rudyard Kipling?"

"I think it came in yesterday with some other books that a customer dropped off to sell," said Keith, rummaging in a shopping bag on the floor. "Yes, here it is."

"Why are you looking so furtive?" Hodge demanded of the customer. "You look like you're buying pornography, and I know we don't carry that here. We don't even have any romance novels unless you count the classics like *Jane Eyre*, which in my view is overrated and overwritten."

"Nice kitty," said the customer. To Keith, he added, "I know Kipling was a raving imperialist with terrible ideology, and an apologist for British imperialism. I'm a leftist. I should hate him, but some of the short stories and poems just make me happy. My whole family cringes every time I get drunk and sing 'The Road to Mandalay' at parties, but I love the lyrics."

"'On the road to Mandalay,
Where the flyin'-fishes play,
An' the dawn comes up like thunder outer China 'crost the Bay!'" quoted Keith sympathetically.

"Wait," said Hodge, his eyes widening. "Fish play? Fish can FLY?"

The customer paid for the book, thanked Keith, stuffed the book hastily into his deep coat pocket, and then seemed to recall himself and asked whether Keith had anything on the Russian Revolution. Soon he was settled happily in a chair in the front alcove near the history section, deep in another book.

Hodge turned back to the computer keyboard and typed: "What's this about fish flying and playing? Do they really do that? Fish sandwiches will never pass these lips again if…"

"There is such a thing as a flying fish," said Keith.

"Well, let's get some for the bookstore so I can play with them!" exclaimed Hodge, typing fiercely.

"They wouldn't survive long out of water," explained Keith.

"Wait," said Hodge, his eyes widening. "Fish play? Fish can FLY?"

"We could leave the sink full, and they could use the john if we kept it impeccably clean," protested Hodge. "And then when they got bored or depressed we could take them down to the Lake—it's only about half a mile away and we can see it out the window. And I could play with them there."

"Hodge, I have work to do, and we are not getting any flying fish," said Keith.

"I wish I had a whole island full of fish," typed Hodge, looking wistful.

"Dream on," said Keith.

....

Keith arrived at the bookstore half an hour early the next morning, greeted Hodge, and locked the door again while performing some domestic tasks in the next room. Hodge followed him and purred approvingly, "There is nothing quite like starting a new day with a pristine cat box and a brimming bowl of fresh kibble. Thank you, Boss Man. You're coming along nicely."

"Soon I'll be able to go into service at Downton Abbey," muttered Keith, who had caught the drift of Hodge's sentiments from their general context.

"Too early in the morning for sarc—" miaowed Hodge, interrupted by a brisk knock on the glass door. "Hold your horses!" he exclaimed over his shoulder, as Keith headed over to the front room to see who it was.

The man at the door was tall, thin, middle-aged, and conservatively dressed. Keith unlocked the door and invited him in.

"Thank you and good morning," said the visitor. "Is that your cat?"

"Does no one bother doing basic research anymore?" demanded Hodge. "Of course I'm his cat. I'm Hodge."

"Yes, that's Hodge," said Keith. "He lives here."

Hodge braced himself for the inevitable "nice kitty," but the visitor merely stared at him with an impersonal intensity that made Hodge wonder if the strange man was in fact some kind of cat.

"May I speak with you privately for a few minutes?" asked the man.

"You can say anything in front of Hodge," Keith replied. Hodge

"And then when they got bored or depressed we could take them down to the Lake—it's only about half a mile away and we can see it out the window. And I could play with them there."

struggled briefly to decide whether this was a compliment or an insult and quickly gave up the effort.

The man looked startled, but made a polite effort to conceal it. "I meant," he said, "in the absence of other humans."

"The customers should start arriving soon, but we'll have a few minutes by ourselves," said Keith.

"Please allow me to introduce myself," said the man, extending a business card to Keith. "I'm James Brown, solicitor to Lady—"

"Marmalade? Gaga?" demanded Hodge.

"Is your cat always this talkative?" asked the man.

"Not usually," said Keith. The man looked pleased—more so than the prospect of an interview without feline vocal accompaniment should have warranted. "The breed tends to be active but quiet," he murmured.

"The breed? Hodge came from the pound."

"Which pound?" said the stranger, looking excited.

"Is your cat always this talkative?" asked the man.

"Chicago Animal Care and Control," chorused Hodge and Keith, catching a sidelong glance at each other in increasingly suspicious bewilderment at this strange inquisition. Hodge began washing his paws.

"And may I ask when you adopted him?"

Keith, now thoroughly rattled, examined the man's business card. It was made from heavy, expensive cream-colored paper, on which was printed

Cholmondeley and Brown
Solicitors
13 Ramsbottom Close
London W2,
United Kingdom

"We adopted him in March of 2009," said Keith.

The man beamed joyfully at Keith and Hodge. "I have reason to believe that your cat 'Hodge' is my client's cat—a purebred Korat from a line of champions, abducted in early kitten-hood by an unscrupulous ex-husband and abandoned at the pound," he said to Keith. "And he has just been gifted with a small, privately owned island in the Indian Ocean. It's not on the map but is known informally to its handful of local residents as 'The Island Full of Fish.'"

. . . .

Keith and Hodge stared at Mr. Brown, speechless.

"There's just one more thing to check," said Mr. Brown. "My client mentioned that her kitten had 'an adorable white spot' on his belly." He reached across the desk and poked inexpertly at Hodge, who immediately recoiled, puffed up and laid his ears back.

"You think you have *droit de seigneur* just because you're a servant of the ruling classes?" demanded Hodge.

"Um, perhaps I can verify it by looking underneath him," said Mr. Brown, unperturbed, crouching rather awkwardly on the floor and peering up at Hodge's undercarriage, ignoring a trio of bewildered customers who had just opened the door and were trying to make their way around him in the narrow space between the desk and the bookshelves on the south wall. "Yes! That's it—a white patch. This is little Wriothsley."

"How do you spell that?" asked Hodge, still ruffled, but with his fur beginning to subside. "It sounds like 'Rizzly,' but no sane person could have named a kitten like me anything that dumb. I was born litter-trained and fluent in three languages."

"I think it would be best if we continued calling him 'Hodge' and recognizing that he's my cat now and he belongs to the bookstore," cautioned Keith, "but tell me more about this 'island full of fish,' and how you found us, and why you're so certain he started life as this kitten named...Risley? And who is your client?"

"Of course," said Mr. Brown graciously. "I'm sure you have legal rights of ownership, and in any case, my client made it clear that if I ever found the cat I was to respect his current custodial arrangements as long as I found him in a good home. My client is Lady Anne Lupo."

"The singer?" exclaimed Keith.

"Exactly," said Mr. Brown. "Here's her photograph," he added, turning on his mobile phone and showing it to Keith and Hodge. The woman in the photo was startlingly beautiful—slender and rather petite, not young, with long ash blonde hair, enormous hazel eyes with thick, sooty lashes, and an amused expression veiling something darker and more melancholy.

"That dame is even better looking than Jane Birkin!" exclaimed Hodge.

"The Island Full of Fish has been in Lady Anne's family ever since the British conquest of the Indian subcontinent, and recently passed into her possession upon the death of her mother in extreme old age," continued Mr. Brown. "Lady Anne is deeply embarrassed by the manner in which the island came into her family, and was planning to donate it to the Communist Party of India, but fell out with the leadership over political differences too arcane for me to understand even after she spent an hour explaining them to me over lunch at Claridge's. It was during our third bottle of wine..."

Hodge and Keith observed that the solicitor, having straightened up and perched on the edge of the desk, was staring meditatively out the window at the lake.

"Yes?" prompted Hodge.

"Nice kitty," said Mr. Brown. "After our third bottle of wine," he resumed, "Lady Anne announced that 'really, it would make more sense to give the island to my cat than that bunch of fake left tails.'"

"People in England wear false tails and pin them off to the side?" exclaimed Hodge.

"Bunch of what?" asked Keith, perplexed.

"Sorry, it's Trotskyist jargon," said Mr. Brown. "You must forgive me—I'm rather jet-lagged and this has been a long search. In any case, having accidentally reminded herself of the sad fate of little Wriothsley, Lady Anne called for a fourth bottle of wine, over which we began speculating as to the possibility that that rotter, her former husband, might have been toying with her when he claimed to have given her kitten to the pound—or whether, perhaps even if he had done that, the cat, as he would be now, might be alive and traceable.

"By the end of the meal, we had agreed that I would undertake to find out. My research on the subject over the past six months has taken me to some strange and unsavory places, but an article in the *Chicago Reader* with a full-page photo of Wrioths—of 'Hodge' brought me here, after Lady Anne saw it and swore it must be the same cat. Lady Anne is, as you will have gathered from her musical performances, highly intuitive and a genius," he finished, flushing slightly.

Hodge rose, stretched, and strode across the desk to the computer keyboard, where, to the astonishment of Mr. Brown, he typed rapidly with his nose and paws: "BUT WHAT ABOUT THE ISLAND FULL OF FISH?"

• •

"Has he always done this?" demanded Mr. Brown.

"For the past year or so," said Keith. "He also keys in YouTube videos and rewrites the lyrics."

"Lady Anne insisted he was special, and of course he grew up in a musical household, but this is a new one to me," said Mr. Brown. "Where did he learn written English?"

"He grew up here surrounded by books, and he seems to have memorized *Wuthering Heights*," said Keith. "I doubt that he did that before he got here—he was only about 10 weeks old when I adopted him."

"I knew him before that," said Mr. Brown, gazing fondly at Hodge. "I met you several times at Lady Anne's place before her execrable ex-husband made off with you. Do you recall any of that?" he asked Hodge.

Hodge thought for a moment, then typed in the address for a YouTube video of Paul Simon singing "Late in the Evening," and switched back over to Word and continued typing, his tail switching back and forth in time to the lively instrumentation:

> *First thing I remember I was perched on someone's head,*
> *Till I tired of that and climbed down to his shoe.*
> *We took a turn around the store,*
> *And then I hopped onto the floor,*
> *And decided that my newfound digs would do,*
> *And it was here in the bookstore,*
> *And I don't remember you.*

"That squares with my recollection," reported Keith. "He'd been here for about a week. I was shelving books and I overheard someone behind me say, 'I've never seen a cat do that. I've seen a *monkey* do that...' He had planted himself on top of a customer's head."

"Do I have to ask you again about the Island Full of Fish?" typed Hodge. Both men were now tapping their feet in time to Simon's irresistible faux-Latin rhythms.

"The Island Full of Fish is a veritable paradise, which you and your new owners will have to visit," said Mr. Brown.

Hodge gazed briefly at Mr. Brown, then typed, "Does it have flying fish?"

"Lots," said Mr. Brown, "especially if you go out in a small boat and sail or row around the island. They fly into the boat. It's kind of a nuisance, actually."

"Let's pack up and go there tonight, Boss Man!" typed Hodge.

"Hodge, Gail and I have responsibilities. We can't just pick up and head off to the Indian Ocean," said Keith, looking wistfully out the window at the heaps of blackened snow piled up in Grant Park.

"I'm sure you'd be more than welcome to visit any time you can once Hodge takes title to the island, and even before," said Mr. Brown. "In the meantime, perhaps Hodge could pay a brief visit to the place on his own? Lady Anne would love to host him and I'd be honored to escort him there on the plane."

"Does she have a private jet?" typed Hodge.

"Heavens, no," said the solicitor. "Lady Anne is so skint that I've done most of this research pro bono. She lives in a tiny bed-sit in Kensington, and hopes to have occasional visiting privileges at the island once she has signed it over to you. We'd be traveling coach class and I'd have to carry you on with me in a piece of soft luggage."

"As long as I have something to read, I can deal," responded Hodge. "Cats are reputed to self-sedate when travelling by air, so it would have to be something like...I don't know, Boss Man, maybe Trollope?"

"This is all happening way too fast," protested Keith, as Mr. Brown countered, "Maybe, but considering our destination and all the fish involved, have you thought of *Moby-Dick*?"

. . . .

"Did you have any evidence that Hodge was left at the pound in Chicago, as opposed to somewhere else, besides Lady's Anne's 'intuition'?" demanded Keith, eager to steer the conversation in a more practical direction and still not fully certain of Mr. Brown's bona fides.

"Her swine of an ex-husband sent us an email full of clues, got up like an ancient riddle," said Mr. Brown. "We couldn't make any sense of it. He talked about a city of ice and fire where the river runs backwards and there are green lights underground, parrots squawking overhead, and falcons clinging to the cliffs. He said it had been ruled for many years by a dynasty wielding a clout. The parrots seemed like the only solid clue so I spent several futile months doing research in the tropics before Lady Anne saw the *Reader* article and pointed out that the Chicago River had been diverted to run backwards. Lady Anne knows everything," he added, without apparent irony.

"I think he was referring to our extreme weather, Lower Wacker Drive, the Daleys, Harold Washington's monk parakeets, and peregrine falcons," typed Hodge. "Seems pretty transparent to me."

"I'm a Londoner," pleaded Mr. Brown.

"What became of this ex-husband?" asked Keith.

"After Lady Anne left him, besides absconding with Hodge he embarked on a career of petty crime in which he stole from the poor, claiming he was modeling himself on Robin Hood, but in reverse," said Mr. Brown. "He eluded the police for several months but was eventually killed when a wasp flew in through a broken window where he was burglarizing a council flat, and stung him. He had an allergic reaction and died instantly."

"In the summertime I catch wasps here in the bookstore if they fly in through the window, and eat them for breakfast," Hodge reported, typing. "It's fun. And this is poetic justice. If that sleazeball had made me his partner in crime he'd be alive today. Although, all things considered, I'm glad he didn't. Pack my bags, Boss Man—I have a play date with a flying fish."

• • • • • • • • • • • • • • • • • • • •

It had finally taken an interview with Lady Anne Lupo via Skype—which Hodge had installed on Keith's computer while Keith and Mr. Brown were arguing about the relative merits of Melville and Patrick O'Brian—for Keith to accept that Hodge really was Lady Anne's former cat, and that it would be safe to release Hodge into Mr. Brown's custody for a week-long winter vacation on the island.

Lady Anne had recognized Hodge instantly and exclaimed, "I'm afraid the joy is too great to be real!" and Hodge had howled ecstatically, "I love people who quote spontaneously from *Wuthering Heights*! And you're even better looking on Skype."

Mr. Brown had explained to Lady Anne that Hodge could understand English but that they would need some sort of tablet computer—or, at least, an old portable typewriter—to enable the cat to communicate by typing. Lady Anne had agreed to let Hodge use the old Remington on which her famous war correspondent father had typed his dispatches for *The Week* in the 1930s. Now Mr. Brown and Hodge were on a plane flying over the Pacific Ocean, having stopped to refuel in Los Angeles.

"Are you OK down there?" asked Mr. Brown, peering into the cat carrier under the seat in front of him, where Hodge was neatly stowed. "Do you want anything?"

"I'm fine," miaowed Hodge reassuringly. "Just a bit sleepy. They weren't kidding when they said cats self-sedate when they're flying. I'm

"Are you OK down there?"

having trouble keeping my eyes open." He narrowed his eyes briefly at Mr. Brown, signifying contentment, and when Mr. Brown continued to peer at him solicitously he began to purr loudly. Mr. Brown smiled, relaxed, and opened his third bottle of airline wine, noting aloud that it was French and perfectly decent.

Mr. Brown's interchange with Hodge had drawn no reaction from the young woman in the next seat, who had gotten on the plane at LAX and had her headphones on, but to Mr. Brown's surprise he heard a loud, raucous miaow emerge from under the seat in front of her. "Hodge?" he exclaimed, but when he checked on Hodge again he saw that Hodge appeared to be asleep.

Hodge was dreaming about a boat full of flying fish when he was awakened by a throaty, anxious appeal almost in his ear.

"Does anyone have any catnip? They gave me cat tranquilizers before

Hodge was dreaming about a boat full of flying fish.

we left, and as usual they've backfired and I'm about to jump out of my skin," the voice said.

"Hey, are you Siamese?" asked Hodge. "Where are you?"

"I'm under the seat next to you, and yes, I'm Siamese," the voice miaowed back.

"I don't have any catnip but I could read to you if that would help you relax," said Hodge, now fully awake. "You might want to dial down the volume a little though, doll. You have a beautiful voice but you sound like Edith Piaf, and some humans are such philistines that they might complain. What's your name?"

"I'm called Ming," said the Siamese apologetically. "Not very imaginative, I'm afraid."

"It's lovely," said Hodge. "Settle down and listen to this, kid. You'll feel better. I'll have to purr it over, though, because sustained miaowing is frowned upon on long-haul flights."

"Thank you," said Ming. "What is it you're going to read to me?"

"It's a novel full of fish," replied Hodge. Clearing his throat slightly, he purred, "'Call me Ishmael,'" and soon he was lost in the narrative, so interested that he was able, although barely, to stay awake and keep reading.

"How are you doing, doll?" he asked after about half an hour.

"Mmmmm," purred Ming. "So much better. Sleepy now. Thinking about fish. Please keep reading, Ishmael."

"I'm actually named—" began Hodge, then thought better of it as he heard Ming yawn, hugely and languorously, and then began to detect the slight, rhythmic wheeze of a cat snore from her carrier.

"That was my good deed for the day," he said. "It seems like the meds those idiots gave her have worn off. Nap time for Hodge."

• •

Several hours later, the plane having crossed most of the Pacific Ocean, the cats were still comfortably asleep in their carriers. Mr. Brown was slumped in his chair sleeping off the copious amount of surprisingly potable airline wine he had drunk, dreaming about Lady Anne Lupo, when his dream began to morph into something disagreeable. Eventually he opened his eyes and understood why: his seatmate, the young woman who had gotten on at LAX, was awake, staring vacantly into space, her headphones on, singing along loudly and tunelessly to Lady Gaga.

The woman seemed familiar. Sleep-fogged and jet-lagged, Mr. Brown stared at her blearily, mentally comparing her vacant and somewhat porcine appearance with Lady Anne's mature, delicate, Sephardic beauty and air of luminous intelligence. The woman shifted position, saw him looking at her, and scowled.

"Have you got a problem, Grandpa?" she demanded, in a bad imitation of an upper-class accent, removing her headphones.

"As a matter of fact, I do," bridled Mr. Brown. "While I have the utmost respect and admiration for Chelsea Manning in her capacity as a whistle-blower, I expect she must have been the office-mate from hell if she sounded anything like you when she was singing along with Lady Gaga."

"Chelsea Handler did what?" asked the young woman, looking confused.

Mr. Brown sighed. "Never mind, madam," he said, "but will you kindly sing in silence, if sing you must, for the rest of the flight?"

The woman muttered something that shocked even Mr. Brown, a man of the world, then rose awkwardly from her cramped seat, knocking her headphones onto the floor and accidentally kicking Ming in her carrier, and stalked off down the long aisle toward the ladies' room at the end of the plane, bumping into several sleeping passengers who had their heads or feet sticking out. More fastidious than gallant, Mr. Brown reached down to pick up the headphones, but saw that a small, pink Hello Kitty notebook had also fallen to the floor. He picked it up, was about to place it on the seat next to him, but then impulsively opened it and began to read the contents. His eyes widened.

"Watch accent. Lady Anne Lupo, not Lupa. Died all alone and forgotten, six months ago. Don't forget to feed Ming. Nuisance cat but must look posh. You are love child only daughter and heir to Island Full of Fish. <u>STAY IN CHARACTER.</u> Remember what Roger said."

Mr. Brown pocketed the notebook.

• •

Ming had been sleeping deeply in her carrier when her owner kicked her. She awoke and moaned softly, waking Hodge.

"What's the matter, kid?" he yawned.

"I don't know," said Ming. "I didn't mean to wake you but my new owner kicked me. She's dangerous. I think she went somewhere but I'm worried about when she comes back."

"What! If she bothers you I'll bite her and Mr. Brown will deal with her," said Hodge. "He seems a little stuffy but he likes cats, and he and I have an understanding."

"My old owner was like that," sighed Ming.

"Your old owner?"

"I was stolen," miaowed Ming, desolately.

"You were kidnapped from a rich family?" asked Hodge, sympathetically.

"No, she and this sleazy guy named Roger stole me from a homeless person when we were sleeping rough near Victoria Station," said Ming. "I loved my owner. He lost his job and his flat but he took me with him when he went to live on the street, and I caught mice and rats for our dinner. Though for some reason he always insisted that I eat them myself. I think he was just trying to be independent," said Ming. "I hope he's all right. I miss him."

"Damn, kid, I'm impressed!" said Hodge. "I came from the city pound but I've always had it easy."

"Is it nice having Mr.—Mr. Brown?—for an owner?" asked Ming.

"Oh, he's not my owner, just my escort," said Hodge. "My owner has a bookstore in Chicago. We're visiting a friend of Mr. Brown's who has given me an Island Full of Fish. It's a long story."

"An Island Full of Fish!" exclaimed Ming. "That's where we're going. The woman who stole me says she inherited the island when her mother died."

"WHAT! When did her mother die?"

"Six months ago, she says. I'm not sure I believe any of it. I overheard her talking about it with her scuzzball friend Roger a long time ago, when he was still alive, and it sounded like they were making up some kind of plot. I forget the mother's name but she was a titled lady."

"Lady Anne Lupo is very much alive. We talked to her by Skype a few days ago in Chicago," said Hodge. "This thing stinks like a big pile of dead fish."

"Will YOU SHUT UP!" demanded a voice above them, as the young woman who had been seated next to Mr. Brown on the plane returned from the ladies' room, trailing a scent of heavy perfume, toothpaste and unwashed clothing. "You damned cat. I'm going to ask the attendant to put you in the baggage compartment for the rest of the flight."

"The baggage compartment isn't climate controlled!" wailed Ming. "Cats can die of cold in there. Ishmael," she quavered, more quietly, "I'm really glad we met. If I don't survive, thank you for your kindness."

"My name is Hodge and you aren't going anywhere!" miaiowed Hodge, even more loudly than Ming. He reached out his paw, unzipped the mesh panel in his carrier, and hopped briskly into Mr. Brown's lap, from which he received the young woman with his usual disconcerting green stare as she squeezed uncomfortably into her seat. "You need to lay off the potato chips, sister, and practically everything else, I expect," he miaowed at her. "Haven't you read about the obesity crisis in the developed world?"

"Shut your cat up and put him back in his carrier!" the woman hissed at Mr. Brown.

"I want a word with you," replied Mr. Brown. "We'll be landing soon, and you'll have to explain to the authorities why you are pretending that Lady Anne Lupo is dead and that you're her love child. I happen to have met her love child, and she looks nothing like you, and her relations with Lady Anne are perfectly cordial. Lady Anne is fine, though it might have taken a while for the people on the island to find that out, since she takes a hands-off approach to her ownership of the place. But I've got you now. You'll have to confess that the aim of this impersonation was nothing less than to steal the Island Full of Fish."

The woman flushed, then turned very pale. "Warlock!" she breathed. "Help!"

"I'm not practicing witchcraft, just detection," retorted Mr. Brown. "I know where I recognize you from. You were a protégé of Lady Anne's despicable ex-husband, Roger. I caught the two of you mugging a pensioner on a housing estate. I punched Roger in the face and I chipped your tooth, which I see you never had fixed," he added triumphantly.

Mr. Brown and his seatmate had been so absorbed in their confrontation that they hadn't noticed that the plane was descending rapidly and expertly through the clouds toward the airport. A flight attendant appeared over their shoulder, reached over to collect Mr. Brown's impressive collection of empty wine bottles, and told them to stow their trays upright and put their cat back in his carrier.

Hodge caught a ravishing glimpse of shining ocean out the window before slipping back into his carrier, then returned his attention to the argument above him. Mr. Brown was saying, "It doesn't take too much imagination to know what you were planning to do with the Island Full of Fish. There's a huge market for fish in Japan, and the island is a beautiful, unspoiled place. You were planning to harvest all the fish and sell them to the Japanese, and then cover the beachfront with jerry-built timeshare condos and cheap hotels!" His voice had risen to a roar.

The plane landed. The flight attendant cautioned passengers to remember to take all their belongings with them, and to queue politely and not push past the people ahead of them. The woman unbuckled her seatbelt, grabbed her handbag, and raced down the aisle to the exit, elbowing everyone else out of her way and finally pushing past the flight attendants and into the passage to the airport.

"Ming, would you like to see the Island Full of Fish with me and Mr. Brown?" asked Hodge. "Because your current owner seems to have taken a powder."

• •

Hodge opened his carrier, and slipped under the seat next to him and unzipped Ming's. "Come on out, doll," he said. Ming emerged from her carrier, blinked, and head-butted him.

"Who is this?" asked Mr. Brown, peering delightedly down at her.

"Give me your phone and I'll explain," miaowed Hodge, pawing at Mr. Brown's pocket where he knew the solicitor kept his phone. Mr. Brown, understanding, produced the phone and turned it on. But when Hodge tried to type on the keyboard, both he and Mr. Brown stared at the results in bewilderment. The screen was a jumble of letters.

"I don't know if I can make my paws and nose work with this thing," complained Hodge. "I'm used to a computer keyboard."

"What are you trying to say?" asked Ming.

"I want to tell him to keep you and take you with us to the Island Full of Fish," said Hodge, "which I'm sure will be fine with him, and fine with Lady Anne."

"We may have to find another way to show him," said Ming. She jumped into Mr. Brown's lap and stared up at him and started to purr.

"I'm drowning in these blue eyes," said Mr. Brown, petting her hesitantly.

"Me too," said Hodge, joining Ming in Mr. Brown's lap.

Mr. Brown continued to look enchanted and flustered.

"We have to somehow let him know that we can't be separated," miaowed Ming.

"This is kind of sudden," said Hodge, "but—I saw this book about a feral cat colony on a Greek island at the bookstore. It was a photo essay on how cats aren't really solitary predators at all. They were all cheek-marking each other and twining their tails together. Maybe…"

Ming leaned against Hodge and twined her long and surprisingly muscular tail around his, and continued to stare at Mr. Brown and purr.

"I can't just leave you here," Mr. Brown told Ming. "Let's put you back in your carrier and we'll take you along to the Island Full of Fish with us." Ming head-butted Mr. Brown, head-butted Hodge again, jumped off Mr. Brown's lap, and slipped into her carrier. Hodge got into his.

"What smart cats," Mr. Brown said. "Hodge, when we get to the island we'll have a typewriter and you'll be able to type again—the keys are about the same size as the ones on your computer keyboard. Now we need to get off this plane." He checked the overhead compartment, found that his seatmate had apparently had no luggage, grabbed his own slender overnight case, and gathered up the cat carriers and zipped the flaps shut. The plane was nearly empty and he made his way easily to the exit, heading with the cats for Immigration Control.

"This part could be kind of tedious," he warned, "but at least I know where my passport and your rabies vaccination and vet records are, Hodge," he said. "We can't have you being sent to quarantine." He patted his jacket pocket, felt the reassuring outline of his passport and the envelope with Hodge's papers, and walked across the airport lobby and got in line, yawning repeatedly as jet lag caught up with him.

Mr. Brown was pleasantly surprised by how short the line was for Immigration Control. The Asian official behind the counter looked at him approvingly and then seemed to freeze for a moment. Recovering his composure, he coolly asked Mr. Brown for his passport, looked it over carefully, and then stamped it. Mr. Brown handed over Hodge's vaccination history, which the man examined and stamped. "Are we free to go now?" asked Mr. Brown.

The official stared at him neutrally. "As soon as you give me the papers for the Siamese," he said, opening Ming's carrier. Ming emerged and beamed at him. He reached out and petted her, smiling for the first time. Mr. Brown looked flummoxed.

"I don't think I have them," he admitted ineffectually. "I packed in a hurry."

"She can't enter the country without them," said the official.

"Are you sure you couldn't make an exception, just to keep the family together?" asked Mr. Brown, who immediately realized this had not been the right thing to say, as the official flushed scarlet.

"I overstayed my visa in the United States and was deported back here. I haven't seen my wife and daughter in five years. And you want me to just wave you through Immigration Control because you have cute cats," he snorted.

"That's terrible!" miaowed Ming, jumping into the official's lap and beginning to purr anxiously.

"Are you acting?" asked Hodge.

"Certainly not!" said Ming. "It's awful being separated from your humans."

The official scratched Ming behind her ears, appreciatively. "Siamese cats are so sensitive," he observed. He looked up at Mr. Brown, and his expression darkened again.

"You western tourists," he said bitterly. "The sex tourists are the absolute worst, but the hippies who come here looking for enlightenment aren't any good either, and then there are the hedonists who think they've found paradise just because it's warm in the winter. When I saw you at a distance I thought, at last, someone has come to our country to conduct himself like a gentleman, even if the handkerchief in his jacket pocket is a bit loud. And then you come up to the counter and I see that it isn't a handkerchief at all. You're a grown man and you're flaunting a hot pink Hello Kitty notebook!"

Mr. Brown, feeling progressively more stupefied by jet lag, reached up and pulled the forgotten notebook out of his pocket. It fell open and revealed a coupon from Macy's for a free gift with the purchase of $27 worth of makeup, at which the official stared stonily. Mr. Brown rifled through the pages and produced a sheaf of papers that turned out to be Ming's vaccination history. He handed it to the official, adding, "The notebook is my daughter's. She was helping me pack. She's a teenager."

The official relaxed. "So is mine," he confided. "I can never understand the faddish stuff they go in for at that age. OK, you're all set. You need to get back in your carrier, sweetie," addressing Ming, who head-butted him briefly and obeyed. "I'll miss you."

Mr. Brown gathered up his luggage and the carriers, thanked the official, and unzipped Hodge's carrier enough to drop the notebook into it. "If you want a break from Melville, do me a favor and read through that and see what it says," he told Hodge, as he strode off down the airport corridor, carefully balancing the cats.

The official stared after him for a long moment. "Barking mad," he observed to the empty air.

• •

"Ming, you're awfully quiet. Are you still upset about the customs guy's immigration problems?" asked Hodge, as the two cats jostled along in their carriers on their way through the airport to the exit.

"It's just so sad!" miaowed Ming. "He must miss his family so. You saw how he stopped being mean once Mr. Brown claimed he had a teenage daughter, too. It's not fair! We shouldn't even have borders between countries."

"But then the United States could invade Mexico," protested Hodge. "Or worse, Canada could invade the US and make us all act nicer to each other. I'd hate that."

"There's not much of a guarantee of national sovereignty anyway," said Ming bitterly, "except maybe nuclear warheads, and they're a disaster waiting to happen for other reasons."

"Ming," said Hodge slowly, "we have only a week together on the Island Full of Fish. Could you try to put these intractable political issues aside while we're here, and just have fun? Because Heaven knows you deserve it, doll. You've had a hard time."

"OK, Hodge," said Ming peaceably, "I'm your guest. I'll focus on having fun with you. After all," she miaowed, her voice suddenly louder and excited, "we're going to be surrounded by fish! We can catch them and eat them whenever we want to. We can practice reaching into the water and grabbing them and eating them raw, like sashimi—"

"Uh, Ming...I have a problem with that," said Hodge.

"Oh, if they're your fish, of course you can eat them and I'll just watch," said Ming, abashed. "I didn't mean to presume...I mean, it's your island, your fish...I just thought...."

"No, doll, that isn't the issue at all. I don't want to eat them. I want to try to make friends with them. After all, they're kind of like my subjects. You don't acquire something precious and ransack it. And anyway, my Boss Man quoted this poem to me when a customer came in looking for a book by Rudyard Kipling, about how the flying fishes play on the road to Mandalay. If fish play and fish can fly...I mean, I know we can't be vegetarians because we're cats, but at that moment I swore off fish sandwiches from Miller's Pub with extra tartar sauce. And up till then they were the guiding star of my existence!"

"The what?"

"Sorry, I stole the metaphor from Dickens—I mean, they were really good. We had them on special occasions. And OK, maybe once I'm back in Chicago I'll go back on them, but while we're here I don't want anyone hurting any fish, OK? Mr. Brown brought some fancy organic kibble with him, and for all I know Lady Anne has a fully functioning chicken farm, but fish shall not pass my lips while I'm here, and I'd rather they didn't pass yours either, because I can tell you're a mighty huntress."

"OK," said Ming. "There are bound to be a lot of rodents for me to catch anyway. I got really good at that while we were living rough in London."

Hodge thought briefly of the mice he had befriended in Chicago, and decided not to say anything unless the occasion demanded it.

Hodge thought briefly of the mice he had befriended in Chicago.

"You know, Ming, we might be able to find your former owner through Lady Anne," he said. "Because it's obvious you really miss him. Lady Anne normally lives in London—she's just visiting the Island Full of Fish. She has a daughter whom she gets along with. I don't know where the daughter is but I suspect it's London, so either one of them could scout around Victoria Station and see if there's a homeless dude who's missing a Siamese cat."

"WOULD YOU REALLY?" howled Ming, overcome with emotion.

Mr. Brown staggered in surprise. "You OK in there?" he said.

"I'm fine," miaowed Ming, much more quietly.

"Hey, dude," pointed out Hodge, "we've walked right up to a boat. I can smell the sea. And this really hot dame is waving at you—are you awake?"

Mr. Brown, now dangerously jet-lagged, put down the cat carriers and struggled to get his bearings.

"James, we're over here. The packet boat is ready to take off for the island. I came along. Where's Hodge?" said the warm, gravelly, cultured whiskey voice that had bewitched two generations.

Mr. Brown and the cats looked up and saw a small, elegant, very tanned woman in a white linen shift dress and bare feet walking toward them. "Anne!" he exclaimed.

"Get on board," said Lady Anne Lupo. "And take a nap. I figured you'd be an absolute wreck by now—you've come more than halfway across the planet. I'll handle the cat and the luggage, and Jacques and I can sail the boat over."

"There's a second cat," said Mr. Brown, with an ecstatic yawn. "It's a long story."

"How lovely!" said Lady Anne, peering into Ming's carrier and picking it up. "And this other one must be Wriothsley—I mean Hodge. Yes, it's you. Welcome to the Island Full of Fish." She picked up Hodge's carrier and climbed into the boat, then reached out her hand to help Mr. Brown on board.

"I'm letting you out of your carriers just in case we have an accident," she told the cats. "If we capsize, which I highly doubt will happen, we'll all swim for it together. We should be back at the Island Full of Fish in 20 minutes—it's not far. Settle down now and relax." She unzipped Hodge's carrier first, then Ming's. The cats hopped up onto the primitive wooden seat next to her and began to purr. Mr. Brown leaned his head on Lady Anne's shoulder and began to snore. The boat pulled away from the dock and motored slowly out of the harbor.

. . . .

Once the boat was out in the sea, Lady Anne and a darkly tanned old man whom she introduced to the cats as Jacques cut the motor and raised the sails. Ming crouched nervously as the boom swung by overhead. Hodge dodged the boom, resisted the impulse to claw his way up the sail, hopped up on the prow, and peered down into the water, which was calm and surprisingly clear. He could see fish in its depths.

Hodge realized he had never been happier—not when he succeeded in scoring an extra handful of Second Fridays potato chips when no one was looking, nor when he had hitched a ride on a customer's head as a kitten, nor even when Keith had walked through the door of the bookstore and presented him with half a fish sandwich from Miller's Pub, with extra tartar sauce. Had he been asked to consider the issue an hour before, he would have said the apex of his short existence had been the time that he had bitten a customer who was bargaining too aggressively with Keith over the price of a first edition of *Mrs Dalloway*.

Twenty minutes later he was nearly knocked off the prow as Lady Anne and Jacques turned on the motor and lowered the sails. Regaining his grip on the boat, he looked around and got his first glimpse, in the distance, of the Island Full of Fish.

"Hey, kid, will you look at that!" he exclaimed to Ming—but before she could answer, a shoal of winged fish rose from the water and flew into the boat. Mr. Brown awoke and gave a startled yelp as one of them landed in his lap.

"Wow!" howled Hodge, suddenly face to face with an especially large and beautiful specimen. He stared at it, entranced. It stared back, with the innocent astonishment of someone who has never seen a cat. They contemplated each other for a moment and Hodge opened his mouth to say something. The fish, recognizing the architecture of a gaping maw with sharp teeth, instinctively took flight. Hodge leaped into the air, following it without thinking.

"Cut the engines!" yelled Lady Anne. "CAT OVERBOARD."

• •

Hodge's leap followed the arc of the flying fish and ended in a shallow dive into the ocean. His open eyes stung from the salt, but recorded a hazy blue-green beauty around him before he surfaced, coughing and sputtering. Without thinking about it he began to swim toward the pier, enjoying the feeling of the water and the smell of salt, fish, and seaweed, and fascinated by the way his legs and paws looked underwater. His head felt extremely sleek. "I bet I look like an otter," he observed aloud to no one in particular.

It stared back, with the innocent astonishment of someone who has never seen a cat.

Lady Anne, meanwhile, had quickly pulled off her dress and dived in after Hodge. Mr. Brown, still not fully awake, was sitting transfixed in the boat, momentarily blinded by her beauty and relieved that she could still afford such elegant La Perla underwear.

"Anne, he seems to be fine," called Jacques. "I'll turn on the motor again once you two get to shore." Lady Anne and Hodge were now swimming together; once she had reached him she had abandoned her rapid crawl for a decorous sidestroke so she could keep an eye on him while he paddled industriously toward the shore.

Ming hunkered down, looking horrified. "Hodge, please don't drown!" she howled, apparently not hearing Jacques or not trusting his judgment.

"I'm loving it, doll," miaowed Hodge. "You should join us."

"No way am I going in the water," said Ming, sounding relieved but still appalled.

"OK," said Hodge peaceably, "no one will force you to swim, but I'm going to be spending a lot of time working on my dog-paddle. This is heaven."

Ming shuddered eloquently and curled up in Mr. Brown's lap. Mr. Brown watched Lady Anne for a minute, then yawned and fell back to sleep.

Lady Anne and Hodge reached the shore a few minutes later. She stood up and shook herself, brushing her hair out of her eyes; Hodge admired her briefly and then surveyed his own body and marveled at his sleekness. "I look like I just lost ten pounds, except I only weigh nine. I don't know if I'm supposed to groom myself now or wait." He tasted his own fur, found it a bit salty, and noticed that a long piece of seaweed had draped itself elegantly over his back, like a garland. Inspecting it more closely, he was struck by its beauty: it seemed to be made up of a thousand small, reddish flowers, and it smelled of salt and frangipani.

"That's native to the island," said Lady Anne. "It's lovely, isn't it? It doesn't grow anywhere else." She detached the seaweed from Hodge, who promptly pounced on it and carried it off in his teeth.

"OK, it's yours, but we should put it in water," called Lady Anne. "I'll handle that when we get back to the house. The boat is just docking. I need to go see to James; he looks like he's sleepwalking. I don't want him to drop Ming overboard by accident." But Ming, overjoyed at the prospect of dry land, had already jumped onto the pier. Mr. Brown clambered awkwardly after her, lost his footing and plunged fully clothed into the sea.

"The notebook!" yelled Mr. Brown, clinging to the pier because his business suit and shoes made swimming almost impossible.

"What are you talking about?" demanded Jacques, dropping a rope ladder over the side of the boat for Mr. Brown.

Lady Anne reached the pier as Hodge stared after her. "I think that dame must be part cat," he said aloud. "She's so fast and graceful."

"The pink notebook! It's full of information on a plot to steal the island," replied Mr. Brown, clambering awkwardly up the ladder.

"James, that notebook is safe in Hodge's cat carrier," said Lady Anne. "I saw it when I was letting him out. I think you're delirious. Let's get you out of those wet clothes and have a drink, and then you can sleep for 16 hours."

"Here are the carriers and your luggage, landlubber," said Jacques, handing them out of the boat to the waterlogged Mr. Brown. Lady Anne interposed and collected the suitcase and carriers, and her dress, which she slipped into, and the three humans joined Ming on the long walk along the pier back to the beach, where Hodge was waiting for them.

"Ming, I saw fish!" he miaowed. "And we swam through a school of them. And there was a blue thing with lots of legs down in the rocks. I want to try to make friends with it."

"That sounds like a poisonous octopus," said Ming, shuddering. "Try and get some more information about this place before you explore it, OK?"

"Don't you like my island?" asked Hodge.

"I love the island; I'm just not sure about the water," said Ming. "It looks like there'll be plenty to do on dry land."

"True, and one of the first things I need to do is get hold of a keyboard, so I can thank Lady Anne properly and ask a few questions," said Hodge. "And I need to get the notebook back, so I can do what Mr. Brown asked me to, and read it for clues about what your kidnapper may be up to. Oh, and I need to tell Lady Anne about your homeless owner back in London, and see if she can get someone to look for him on the pavement near Victoria Station, so you two can be reunited. Man, I got my paws full!"

The humans had gone on ahead and were filing through the door of a small, weathered old house covered in flowering vines, with fruit trees in the yard.

"My owner's wife would go nuts for this garden," said Hodge. "She has whole rooms full of tropical plants at home. It's like a jungle. My friend Ma'at and I hid in the bushes in the west window of the dining room, and ate half the Thanksgiving turkey, and no one noticed us. I'm waiting for them to find the bones and decide that their spouse is practicing Santeria."

"Who is Ma'at?" demanded Ming suspiciously.

"She's my girlfriend. She's a pain in the ass," confided Hodge, not giving the matter much analysis.

"My owner's wife would go nuts for this garden," said Hodge.

Ming gave him a deep blue stare, which, fortunately, he was too absorbed in sniffing at the air to notice.

"I brought you cats some organic kibble," said Lady Anne as the party crossed the threshold. "There are also a lot of fish around here, but what you do with them is between you and your conscience. That means all four of you; I'm a vegan but I can turn a blind eye in the interest of hospitality. And once I sign this island over to Hodge it will be up to him to decide."

Lady Anne and Jacques sat down on an old Victorian couch that was discretely leaking horsehair, which Hodge began probing intently. Ming perched on the arm of the couch, uncharacteristically aloof. Mr. Brown emerged from the next room, half dry, his hair sticking out wildly, wearing a plain cotton kimono, and joined them, again yawning prodigiously. Lady Anne poured out martinis from a pitcher and handed them around. "To Hodge, and new beginnings," said Lady Anne, and the humans clinked their glasses and drank deeply.

"This feels a lot like home," observed Hodge.

"And please make yourself at home," responded Lady Anne, addressing Hodge. "I've put out kibble for both of you in that corner, and your cat boxes are over here," she said, rising from the couch and pointing to opposite corners of the room. Hodge noted with approval that the corners, and the rest of the room, were not so much dusty as sandy, and that there was a whole wall full of books—though, as he told himself, he was unlikely to have much time to read during his short stay on the island.

"I have a lot of questions to ask you, but first we need to find that old-school computer thing you and Mr. Brown were talking about, so I can type them," he miaowed to Lady Anne. "Those mobile phone keyboards are rubbish. I think the thing we're looking for is called a type-writer or a type/writer?"

"She can't understand cat speech," Ming reminded Hodge.

"I keep forgetting that, doll. Lady Anne is such a goddess I assume she can do everything. Let's wait till after dinner and I can ferret out the device—I've seen photos of them online back in Chicago—and explain. One thing I want to ask her is whether we're free to go out at night, maybe through a window or something. I'd like to see the place and maybe do that Minnaloushe thing, which I never managed to pull off in the bookstore."

"The what?" demanded Ming.

"'Minnaloushe creeps through the grass,
Alone, important and wise,
And lifts to the changing moon
His changing eyes,'"

quoted Hodge. "It's a poem by Yeats about outdoor cats."

"Well, you're arguably important, since you got us here, and you're going to be spending a lot of time alone," muttered Ming under her breath. "But 'wise'? Not bloody likely."

"Hey, that's cute!" exclaimed Hodge. "I didn't know Siamese cats could do that growling, snorting thing. Let's score some of that kibble—I'm starving."

The kibble was delicious and Lady Anne had put out heaping bowls of it, next to a big communal dish of fresh water. As the cats were having their dinner, Lady Anne and Jacques assembled a light, cold supper for the humans, which Mr. Brown ate in hungry and grateful silence before

"Let's score some of that kibble—I'm starving."

waving vaguely at everyone and staggering off to bed. On his way out of the room he paused in front of a framed photo that looked recent.

"Leonie looks more and more like you," he said to Lady Anne. "Give her my love when you see her. That reminds me, tomorrow we need to talk about this woman whose notebook I have who is running around claiming to be her."

"Is this about that 'plot to steal the island' you were talking about earlier?" asked Lady Anne.

"Yes, but I'm too knackered to explain it properly at the moment," said Mr. Brown. "All I can say now is watch out for a fat blonde with an affected accent and terrible manners. I sent her packing on the mainland but she might be stupid enough to try something."

Lady Anne snorted. "Fat, blonde, and stupid is the polar opposite of my daughter. Let's talk about this in the morning. It sounds like a laugh riot. And I'm ready to crash, too. The sun set an hour ago. Cats, we'll see you at breakfast and we can all go for a walk and maybe a swim. Hodge, you and Ming had better stay indoors tonight until you know your way around. I don't know of any natural predators on the island, but, as Mr. Dylan said, 'You always got to be prepared/But you never know for what.'"

"You said it," muttered Ming bitterly, and then, recalling herself, miaowed, "Thank you for everything."

"I'm heading out to the beach for a smoke," announced Jacques. "I'll be back in a few and I'll lock up. Good night, Anne."

Hodge and Ming returned briefly to their kibble. Ming stared in astonished delight at their water dish, in which a full moon was reflected through the window. She reached into the water and patted it, watching the reflection shatter and re-form, then reached under the bowl and tipped it just enough to alter the image without spilling the water. She gave it a tentative push with her nose and piloted it a few inches across the old tiled floor.

"What is this, cat science?" asked Hodge affectionately. "You trying to figure out what's in there?"

"No, it's art," said Ming shortly.

"Speaking of art, look at this portrait!" exclaimed Hodge, gesturing with his tail toward the photo Mr. Brown had commented on. "That dame is even more beautiful than Lady Anne. Your kidnapper was not the brightest bulb in the chandelier. Can you imagine two women who look less alike?"

"No," admitted Ming. "Wrong age—this woman looks older—and wrong race. One's ugly, the other's beautiful, one is dumb as a post... And my kidnapper was as mean as she was stupid, but this woman looks really smart and sensitive, like Lady Anne. She looks familiar. And not just because she looks like Lady Anne. Don't you think? I feel like I've seen that face before."

Hodge stared at the photo. "Me too," he announced. "Now where was it? Probably in the bookstore, since that's where I mainly spend my time...let me think. Maybe the music section? This is going to keep me up all night."

"While you're thinking I'm getting some sleep," replied Ming.

• •

At breakfast the next morning, even Mr. Brown was cheerful and alert after a long sleep, and Lady Anne appeared to be in an extraordinarily good mood. Hodge had awakened to the sound of her singing in the kitchen as the three humans cooked and set the table, and had opined to Ming that "that dame sounds even better than Jane Birkin."

Ming had considered the proposition and remarked "more robust" before remembering how annoyed she was with Hodge, after which she lapsed into a dignified silence for 30 seconds before exploding out onto the porch through the open door after a hummingbird.

The cats and the humans assembled at the table, the cats sitting on straight-backed wooden chairs like everyone else and, still sated with last night's kibble, keeping their paws discretely off the table. Lady Anne handed around coffee. "What is all this about a fat blonde pretending to be Leonie and trying to steal the Island Full of Fish?" she asked Mr. Brown.

"Wait, I can explain," miaowed Hodge. "I heard it all, and there's something else I want to ask you about." He pounded briefly with his nose and paws on the table top, as Ming miaowed sharply, "Table manners!" and Jacques asked, "Did he find a bug?"

"I think he's miming typing," said Mr. Brown. "I explained earlier to

Anne that Hodge can communicate using a computer keyboard, and that he can probably adapt to her father's old typewriter. I'm happy to tell you all about this thieving blonde but I'd just as soon let him explain."

"Here it is," said Lady Anne, getting up and opening a desk drawer and pulling out a vintage Remington. She inserted a piece of paper in it and returned to the table, putting the typewriter in front of Hodge.

Hodge looked at the machine in perplexity, like someone confronted with a smart phone for the first time, then tapped tentatively at the t, h, and e keys. When nothing happened he typed harder, then recoiled from the unfamiliar harsh noise of the key striking the roller through the paper. He tried again, suddenly intent, and eventually stepped back and indicated the resulting sentence with a flourish of his tail. The humans peered past him and read:

"Harder to type, but it sure puts the 'cat' in 'staccato.'"

Ming and the humans groaned. "If you persist in exhibiting this donnish sense of humor I'll tell the story myself," warned Mr. Brown. "In fact, let me sketch out the outline first or we may be here all morning. Anne, on the plane my seatmate was an unpleasant young blonde whom I've already described. After having gratuitously insulted me, she dropped her notebook on the way to the lavatory, and I thumbed through it and found this." Mr. Brown, having recovered the pink Hello Kitty notebook from where he had stowed it in Hodge's cat carrier, showed Lady Anne the incriminating notes: "Watch accent. Lady Anne Lupo, not Lupa. Died all alone and forgotten, six months ago. Don't forget to feed Ming. Nuisance cat but must look posh. You are love child only daughter and heir to Island Full of Fish. **STAY IN CHARACTER.** Remember what Roger said."

"I called her on it and she panicked and elbowed her way off the plane once we landed," continued Mr. Brown. "I let her know that I recognized her from London, where I once saw her with your despicable ex-husband Roger trying to mug a pensioner on a council estate, a robbery that I prevented with properly targeted violence—you may recall Roger spent a few weeks trying to get your sympathy for his two black eyes? Anyway, I don't think she's likely to succeed, but I wanted you to be on your guard."

"What's this about Ming being a 'nuisance cat'?" demanded Lady

Anne. "Ming is a delightful guest."

"THAT FAT BLONDE STOLE MING FROM A HOMELESS GUY SLEEPING ON THE SIDEWALK NEAR VICTORIA STATION," typed Hodge, having unintentionally stepped on the Caps Lock key. "MING MISSES HIM AND WORRIES ABOUT HIM. YOU KNOW ANYONE WHO CAN HELP FIND HIM AND REUNITE THEM?"

"This machine is cramping my style some," he miaowed parenthetically. "But I guess it's tightening it up. I feel like Hemingway." Ming muttered something under her breath.

"My daughter Leonie is staying a short Tube ride from Victoria," said Lady Anne. "While we're out here on the island I could ask her to mobilize our friends to canvass the area looking for Ming's owner. I could even post something on my Facebook fan page once I get back to the UK. Jacques, are you up for another run back to the mainland today so we can get hold of a phone? We don't have satellite coverage out here," she explained to James and the cats.

Hodge looked bewildered, then stunned. "YOU MEAN WE DON'T HAVE A PHONE OR INTERNET ACCESS HERE?"

"That's why we suggested you use the typewriter," explained Mr. Brown. "Are you all right?"

"BUT IF I WANT TO LET THE BOSS MAN KNOW HOW WE ARE AND WHAT'S HAPPENING, WHAT DO I DO?"

"Unless there's an emergency, you can wait till you get home," said Mr. Brown. "We think finding Ming's owner and letting him know she's alive and well and coming back to him is urgent, especially because he needs help."

"Wait," interposed Lady Anne. "It sounds like Hodge is used to keeping a real-time record. Hodge, how about we leave the paper in the typewriter and whenever you want to, you write about your day? And then at the end of the trip, we can either send the paper to your owner by snail mail, or Mr. Brown can hand-carry it with him when he takes you home to Chicago? That way you can keep a log."

"LIKE A BLOG WITH THE FIRST LETTER MISSING?" typed Hodge.

"Exactly," said Lady Anne.

"U GOT IT," typed Hodge.

That afternoon, Mr. Brown and Jacques returned from their short trip to the mainland in the packet boat, with a box of dragon fruit and the news that they had reached Lady Anne's daughter Leonie in London by phone. Leonie thought she knew who Ming's homeless owner was, and promised to head over to Victoria Station later that morning and try to find him.

Hearing this, Ming howled with joy. The humans grimaced and put their hands over their ears. "Siamese really do have a voice on them," observed Hodge. Ming snorted at him and darted out the door after a butterfly.

"I think the sun is over some yardarm somewhere," said Jacques, beginning to assemble the ingredients for martinis. Lady Anne and Mr. Brown put together a plate of cold hors d'oeuvres as Hodge hopped onto the table and began banging away at the keys of the old typewriter.

"Are you sure he isn't going to break that thing?" asked Mr. Brown.

"I think it's indestructible," replied Lady Anne. "My father had it with him all through World War II. Besides, I like hearing the clatter of it in the background—it takes me back."

"Not to World War II," observed Mr. Brown gallantly.

"May I read the rest of what you've written today?" Lady Anne asked Hodge.

"Sure thing, babe," miaowed Hodge, stepping aside as the humans gathered around the typewriter and began to read.

HODGE'S ISLAND LOG

Monday

SPENT THE MORNING CHASING LAND CRABS. LAND CRABS SPENT THE AFTERNOON CHASING ME. THEN I WENT SWIMMING AGAIN AND SAW THAT BLUE THING AND COUNTED ITS LEGS. THERE WERE EIGHT. THINK MING IS RIGHT AND IT'S A POISONOUS OCTOPUS. IT DISAPPEARED INTO A CLEFT IN THE ROCK WHILE I WAS LOOKING AT IT. DID I OFFEND IT? NOT SURE HOW TO APPROACH IT. THE WATER IS VERY CLEAR AND YOU CAN SEE ALL KINDS OF ANIMALS. TRIED TO MAKE FRIENDS WITH FISH. NOT SURE HOW TO APPROACH FISH EITHER.

HODGE

HODGE'S ISLAND LOG, CONTINUED

Tuesday

Dear Boss Man,

Kept my vows not to hurt any fish, but am chowing down on shrimp, crabs (not land crabs), lobsters and shellfish. As long as it comes from the water and doesn't have fins or scales I'll eat it. Ming says I have Jewish dietary law backwards. I told her there were no cats in the Old Testament.

Today I met a catfish in the stream behind the house. I pointed to my whiskers. It looked at me and dove into the mud.

I swam upstream and clambered out to sun myself. Found myself face to face with a walking fish. It ran away on its fins surprisingly fast but I was ahead of it. I said, "Can't we just talk? I want to be friends." It told me I was two tailfins short of a Studebaker. I told it I owned the island and wanted to be a good steward. It leaned toward me on its fins and pronounced that I was a few scales short of a snakeskin. Then it vanished in the undergrowth. Sometimes I feel like no one here understands me. And vice versa.

Hodge

Wednesday

Dear Boss Man,

I take back everything I said about how I would eat anything that comes from the water and doesn't have fins and scales. I was practicing my breaststroke near the beach and suddenly I saw something dive beneath me, and then I was being lifted up in the air. I hung on and heard someone whistle "Watch those claws, dude!" We went flying up and dove back down into the water, and when we surfaced I saw I was riding on the back of a dolphin. We went way out till I could hardly see the beach, and we swam through shoals of flying fish, and Pliny—that's what he said he was called—told me they wouldn't play with him either. We had the best time ever and then he said they'd better take me back before my humans got worried. On the way back I saw this cool triangular fin coming toward us through the water, but Pliny said, "Hang on, that doesn't belong this close to the shore—Hodge, I mean literally **hang on!** *We're going to jump the shark." And before I knew what was happening the whole pod was beating up on the shark and he got scared and swam*

away. They dropped me off in the shallows and I thanked them and went back in the house because Lady Anne was calling me for dinner.
Hodge

Thursday
Dear Boss Man,

Ming hasn't messed with any fish, but since we arrived all the birds and rodents have moved to the other side of the island. I caught the last of the mice on his way out just so I could apologize to him, but I couldn't get any sense out of him so I let him go.
Hodge

Friday
Dear Boss Man,

Ming is still scared of the water and has been spending a lot of time in the woods. Today I followed her and caught up with her in the trees, but before I could ask her how she was enjoying her vacation, this spotted wildcat landed on me and tried to pick a fight. I declined. Ming introduced him as "Felis bengalensis" and said he was an "Asian Leopard Cat." I said that last part was obvious from context. Ming preened herself and said, "Congratulate me. I'm going to have Bengals." Sometimes the stuff that dame says goes right by me.
Hodge

. . . .

Saturday was Hodge's last day on the Island. Mr. Brown had packed their things in advance, planning to get up early and head back to the mainland in the packet boat with Lady Anne and Jacques (who together would be piloting the boat), and then catch the plane back to Chicago, with Hodge in his cat carrier. Lady Anne was planning to return to London a few days later with Ming, and then connect with her daughter Leonie to make sure Ming was reunited with her owner and that he got some housing assistance.

"If he has to move into my bedsit we'll find space for him and Ming somehow," she said generously.

Lady Anne had also promised Hodge to bring the typed log of his adventures back to London, and mail it from there to Keith at the bookstore in Chicago. And she had packed the seaweed in which he had first emerged from the ocean at the start of the trip, and which he insisted was "his," in foil and a linen towel soaked in sea water, and tucked it into a corner of his carrier.

Hodge resumed his place at the typewriter late that afternoon, once Lady Anne had removed the nearly full sheet of typing paper containing his log and replaced it with a fresh one. Hodge immediately got the Caps Lock key stuck again and typed, "ABOUT YOUR GIVING ME FORMAL TITLE TO THE ISLAND FULL OF FISH—COULD YOU JUST HOLD IT IN TRUST FOR ME INFORMALLY? I DON'T SEEM TO HAVE MUCH OF A TALENT FOR RELATING TO FISH."

"Certainly, if you feel that way," Lady Anne told Hodge. "It would be useful to have somewhere to escape to if I end up living in a one-room apartment with Ming and her owner, and possibly Leonie, who never seems to have a fixed address—which makes sense since her band is usually on tour. But please feel free to visit the island any time, and please bring your owners Keith and Gail with you—they sound delightful."

"THANKS A PETABYTE," typed Hodge, who had briefly delved into computer science back at the bookstore before realizing he preferred just using them. He thought longingly for a moment of the ease and fluency with which he could type on the computer keyboard at home in Chicago, then consoled himself that he'd be back there in less than 48 hours.

"Would everyone like to go for an evening swim?" suggested Mr. Brown, who had emerged from the hallway attired in a pair of surprisingly loud floral swimming trunks. The other humans agreed, changed quickly, and headed to the beach, followed by Hodge and Ming. The sun was just beginning to set. It was still quite light, and the water was warm. Hodge paddled along companionably in the semi-shallows with Lady Anne.

"You really rock that bathing suit, sister," he miaowed. "I know chicks a third of your age who would kill for a body like that." Lady Anne, fortunately, understood nothing of this; she smiled indulgently at him and turned lazily on her back and closed her eyes, then swam slowly, parallel to the shore. Hodge was considering jumping playfully onto her chest when a familiar triangular fin appeared in his line of vision, and as he looked down into the translucent water he saw an open maw full of sharp teeth heading for Lady Anne's slim, brown ankle. Hodge half rose from the water, thrashing as he came down again, and then managed to lunge and land on the shark's back. He howled.

Lady Anne was looking around now and treading water, trying to see what the fuss was about. She hadn't seen the shark. Hodge scrambled over the shark's fin and put a paw over each of its eyes, then opened all his claws and dug them in. The shark paused. Lady Anne saw it, yelled "Hodge!" and punched the shark in the nose, treading water. The shark reeled. Lady Anne's educated punches were so fierce and precise that Hodge found it hard to hang on. Giving the shark's eyes a final vicious clawing, he retreated and clung to its fin. He dug his teeth into the fin and tasted raw fish.

"Anne!" screamed Mr. Brown, blasting through the water in a fast, graceless and alarming stroke that Hodge recognized as the "dolphin," which, he thought, did a disservice to his dolphin friend Pliny, who had taught him how to jump a shark just three days earlier. Lady Anne continued punching the shark on the nose, now joined by Mr. Brown and Jacques, who were pounding on it less expertly.

The shark wobbled, dipping Hodge briefly in the water, executed a slow and sloppy turn, and began heading out to sea with Hodge still on its back.

"HODGE, LET GO!" screamed Lady Anne, striking out after the shark as Jacques and Mr. Brown grabbed clumsily at her feet to stop her. Hodge dug his teeth in as hard as he could and ripped away half the shark's fin. The shark seemed to stagger underwater, then continued swimming, more slowly and erratically. Hodge dropped off its back with the fin still in his mouth.

Lady Anne, muttering something shocking under her breath, reached Hodge in a few fast strokes, and he jumped onto her back instinctively and rode to shore. "Did you learn that crawl for the Olympics?" he demanded, through a mouthful of shark's fin.

Lady Anne and the men collapsed on the sand, staring out to sea. Hodge began chewing on the shark's fin in earnest. "This is superb!" he miaowed. "Guilt-free sashimi!"

"Ugh, I can't watch," called Ming fastidiously. "But I'm glad you're alive."

"I'm not going to stop till I finish this," Hodge miaowed.

"I think we all need to dry off and have a stiff drink," said Jacques. "And once the cat stops amusing himself with the shark's fin we can put it in the icebox and make some bootleg shark's fin soup tomorrow."

"IT'S MINE!" howled Hodge.

"I don't think he'll give it up," said Lady Anne. "And he saved my life a minute ago. If he wants to eat it he can have it. I can put what he doesn't finish now in the fridge, and he can have it later."

"I WANT IT NOW," miaowed Hodge, whose rhetoric had not been improved by typing in all capitals on the typewriter.

"I don't think you can get it away from him," said Mr. Brown. "I suggest drinks and dinner on the porch, and the hero of the hour can keep working away at it in the background."

"It looks like it's about a fifth of his body weight," said Lady Anne doubtfully, "but they're carnivores, so maybe it will be all right. And I trust his judgment." Ming looked at her incredulously but kept quiet.

Many hours later, Hodge had finished the shark's fin and crawled into his carrier. He was so deeply asleep that the laughing, singing, and dancing of the humans, and Ming's enthusiastic caterwauling, barely reached him. He awoke briefly at dawn to find himself being loaded onto the packet boat in his carrier, then fell asleep almost immediately. He surfaced for a moment at the airport, then woke again high over the Pacific Ocean, and looked up to see Mr. Brown smiling out the window with a full wineglass in his hand.

"Soon be home," Hodge purred to himself, then slipped even deeper into the healthy self-sedation of an airborne cat who has recently eaten a quarter of his own body weight.

A HERO'S WELCOME

"Of course he's breathing! I'd know if he were dead," said Gail irritably into the phone.

"Yes, he does smell. Of fish! He stole four fried fish sandwiches from a customer and Keith couldn't get them away from him.

"No, Keith is not scared of his own cat. Apparently Hodge did a vertical leap into the rafters and wouldn't come down, and anyway Keith is trying to run a business and had other things to deal with. Right. Thank you." She hung up the phone. "Is it my imagination or is Dr. Smith getting snarkier with age?" she asked Keith.

"He's a good vet," said Keith. "He probably thinks we're turning into one of those neurotic Hyde Park couples who bring their cat in for observation every time it sneezes. So what did he tell you?"

"He said Hodge will wake up eventually, and that we might be able to enter him in the Guinness Book of World Records for the longest uninterrupted sleep in the history of the species."

Ma'at approached Hodge and licked his face tenderly, then swallowed the fugitive flake of fish that had been hanging from the corner of his mouth, licked her lips, and began to purr.

"If we're lucky maybe he'll never wake up," muttered Keith.

"Dream on," said Gail.

"Thank you, but I've had a most refreshing sleep," mumbled Hodge, beginning to stir. He opened his eyes, yawned prodigiously and staggered to his feet. "Saving lives is hard work, and shark's fin is extremely filling," he miaowed. "As you can see, I'm still digesting it. Hence my temporary dolphin-like appearance." He stared appreciatively at his distended furry belly. "I take it you missed me?"

"Well, finally came the dawn," replied Keith sarcastically.

Hodge ambled over to the computer on the table and began to type.

"I realize you don't know that I jumped a shark that was closing in on the divine Lady Anne Lupo. I saved her life. You'll find out about that in a month or two when you get her letter from London with my travel diary. But even so I would expect a warmer welcome after I've spent a whole week on the other side of the world, in the Indian Ocean on the Island Full of Fish."

Keith and Gail read this and stared at each other.

"Is this what they call the insanity defense?" asked Ma'at.

"WHAT'S ALL THIS ABOUT FISH SANDWICHES?" typed Hodge. Now half-adapted to typing on Lady Anne's father's old Remington, he had managed to tread on the computer keyboard's Caps Lock key. "I'M OFF FISH SANDWICHES NOW. FISH ARE MY FRIENDS. LET ME TELL

"Thank you, but I've had a most refreshing sleep."

YOU HOW I SPENT MY WEEK ON THE ISLAND FULL OF FISH."

Keith snorted explosively. "If that's how you treat your friends, how do I get on your enemies list?" he asked. "You stole a bag of fish sandwiches and ate all four of them in 15 minutes!"

"I WASN'T HERE. I was in transit, flying back from the island with Mr. Brown," protested Hodge, having eventually managed to disengage the Caps Lock key. "Have you taken leave of your senses, Boss Man? Just what do you think happened yesterday?"

"Yesterday," said Keith, "was a very eventful day. Hodge, are you paying attention? Because you seem to be experiencing some kind of lost weekend."

"'Eventful'?" chorused Gail and Ma'at (the latter chirping), curious.

"Is it too early for a martini? It's my day off," said Keith plaintively.

"I'm sure the sun is shining over some yardarm somewhere," typed Hodge. "Hang on a minute," said Gail, vanishing into the kitchen and emerging a few minutes later with a pitcher and glasses. "Thanks," said Keith, draining half of his.

"Yesterday," he said, staring into the thicket of flowering plants in the west window, "began when that kid who credits Hodge with fixing his broken love life showed up with his girlfriend and a bag of fish sandwiches from Miller's Pub. He announced that they were getting married, and to celebrate he had brought a sandwich for each of us, including Hodge.

"Hodge interrupted my congratulations by grabbing the bag of sandwiches from the guy and leaping up onto the top shelf," Keith continued. "The guy and his girlfriend thought that was hilarious, fortunately. I tried to climb up and get the sandwich bag away from you, Hodge, but you did your snarling feral cat imitation. By then the heating system was acting up and I had to open a window to cool the place off.

"I didn't have a chance to put the screen down, and suddenly a flock of seagulls flew in and were all over the place, and making a hell of a racket. Two of them flew up and grabbed the empty sandwich bag, which was a relief, since I didn't want to have to climb up there and clean up after you. We shooed them all out the window, which took about half an hour, and then one of them dropped the empty bag and it landed on a cop's head on the sidewalk. I jumped back before he could see me and think I'd done it.

"By then you had clambered down and were snoring in your cat bed on the desk. I was thinking we might get some peace for five minutes, when a pleasant British customer in a well-tailored suit showed up looking for a first edition of *The Portrait of a Lady.* I was just wrapping it up for him when Anna Wolf's nephew showed up in the doorway with a huge crate which he said was 'for Hodge.' He said Dr. Wolf had died recently—she was over a hundred—and had included a case of canned tuna for you in her will. You remember her—that portly, eccentric old customer who was so fond of you?"

. . . .

"So you're telling me it was all a dream?" typed Hodge. "That I was asleep after purloining this guy's fish sandwiches, but still registering the events around me? Anna Wolf became Lady Anne Lupo, the flying fish were seagulls, the British customer looking for Henry James became the British solicitor James Brown, the case of tuna became title to the Island Full of Fish, AND MY HEROIC BELLYFUL OF MARAUDING-SHARK FIN IS NOTHING MORE THAN AN OVERINDULGENCE IN FISH SANDWICHES FROM MILLER'S PUB." (He had gotten the Caps Lock key stuck again.)

"That sums it up nicely," said Keith.

Hodge abandoned the keyboard and ambled slowly to his cat carrier, his belly swaying gently beneath him. ("Quit staring. I'll digest it in a day or two and be back to normal," he grumbled.) He reached into the carrier, pulled something out, and dragged it back to the keyboard, where he typed, "EXPLAIN THE SEAWEED."

Gail reached out and picked up the trailing garland and examined it. "It does look aquatic, and not local," she said. "It smells like frangipani! I'll put it in water. Maybe it will grow."

"Those reddish flowers are beautiful," Keith admitted. "I wonder where he got it?"

"It seems like it was part of an arrangement—it has some kind of wet rag tied around the roots. Could one of the seagulls have carried it in?" asked Gail. "Not from the lake, but maybe from some discarded bouquet? Or have the paperweight people next door to your office had a fancy reception recently and tossed out the flowers afterwards?" She headed into the kitchen with the seaweed trailing from her hand along the floor.

"THAT'S MINE," howled Hodge, pouncing on it.

"Will you chill out?" demanded Gail. "I'm putting it in water,"

"It can go back to the bookstore if Hodge is so attached to it," she told Keith. "Just keep an eye on it, keep it out of direct sunlight, and I'll see if I can find anything online about how to make it grow indoors. If it's imported it might need some salt in the water, or other nutrients."

"That did not come from a bouquet," snarled Hodge. "It came off me when I was swimming near the Island Full of Fish, and Lady Anne saved it for me." Jumping back on the table, he caught a glimpse of himself in the window and stopped short. "I don't recognize myself," he miaowed plaintively. Not only was he several pounds heavier from the fish he had eaten, but he had puffed up with emotion, and all his fur was standing on end. He approached the computer and began to type, gradually becoming sleek again.

"Look, I'm happy to be back, which is evidence of my magnanimous nature, and also shows how important modern technology is to a happy and successful life. It's hard to express yourself on an old type-writer. But you'll find out soon enough where I was, when you get Lady Anne's letter with my log, and maybe even some photos of me and Ming. Jacques was snapping pictures of us with an old analogue camera. She wants you guys to come out and see the Island Full of Fish. You'll love it.

"And Boss Man, I don't dispute your account of what happened, but I have no memory of it. What we have here is a bookworm hole. Apparently I can be in two places at once. We just have to figure out how it works."

"Who's Ming?" demanded Ma'at, seizing on the only part of this that made sense to her, and seizing Hodge by the tail.

"She's my girlfriend. She's a pain in the ass," said Hodge, absently. "Let go of that."

• •

"Ma'at, will you leave my tail alone!" bellowed Hodge. "I said let go of it."

Ma'at released his tail long enough to ask, "Hodge, what do you mean by 'girlfriend'?"

Hodge tucked his tail quickly beneath him, giving the tip a consoling lick. "I mean whatever dame I'm palling around and getting into trouble with," he said. "What's gotten into you?"

Ma'at looked thoughtful. "But Hodge," she said eventually, "what about love? Looking up to someone? Protecting them and being ready to lay down your life for them?"

"What's that got to do with it?" parried Hodge, thinking suddenly of Lady Anne Lupo and how he had jumped the shark that was closing in on her without a thought for his own safety. He stared at his paws, wondering whether the shark's fin had tasted so sweet because he had torn it off the shark in the process of driving it away from Lady Anne.

Ma'at looked even more thoughtful. "Tell me about Ming?" she finally asked.

"Ming is a Siamese cat I met on the plane, travelling with a woman who had kidnapped her from her owner, a homeless man living outside Victoria Station in London. We went to the Island Full of Fish Together and I helped arrange for Lady Anne's daughter in London to find the guy so they can be reunited. Ming misses her owner terribly. And while we were on the island she spent a lot of time in the forest with some overly aggressive spotted wildcat, and now she says she's 'going to have Bengals,' whatever that means. I wish that broad well but I don't understand half the stuff she says," Hodge concluded wearily.

As Hodge was inspecting his tail for damage, the telephone rang. Gail picked it up, listened, frowned, and said, "But we don't know anyone named Moose and Trixie."

The phone's earpiece emitted what sounded to Keith, across the room, like a distant roar. Gail recoiled from the noise, nearly dropping the phone, and reported, "There's a guy downstairs at the front desk who claims to be your college roommate, but he told me to 'Just let Slugger know we're here.' 'Slugger'?"

"That's what Moose used to call me, for some reason. We'd better invite him up," Keith replied unhappily.

• • • • • • • • • • • • • • • • • • • •

Keith opened the door to the apartment, and admitted a very large couple with a thin, elegantly groomed cream-colored giant poodle and several suitcases.

"We were passing through on our way home to Wisconsin, and we decided to stop here and spend the night with you," said a woman Gail and Keith assumed to be Trixie. The other member of the couple had caught Keith in a crushing hug, and, after replacing Keith's feet on the floor, slapped his back fiercely and said, "Su casa is mi casa, eh, Slugger? Are those martinis? Where's my glass? The little woman is my wife, Trixie, and the dog is Diamond Lil, also known as Di and Delilah."

"That must be why she looks so confused," muttered Gail.

"Poodles have small, dark, close-set eyes in a small face with a long nose," growled the dog. "That trait is also found in certain terriers. It does not make us mentally subnormal. I suspect you have been hanging out with golden retrievers and warping your perspective."

"Di, don't growl at the lady," said Trixie—"Ooh, what a sweet little pussy!" She had noticed Ma'at, who looked at the poodle and at Trixie, then at Trixie's husband, and vanished under the couch.

Hodge strode over to Trixie, placed his paw firmly on her calf, bit her bare ankle, and retreated a few feet. "You don't use that kind of language about my girlfriend," he snarled. "Didn't your mama teach you any manners?"

"What the—" demanded Trixie, bending down to inspect her ankle.

"He's had his shots," said Keith.

"You need to do something about that animal," said Trixie. "Can you lock him up? We'll be here till around noon tomorrow. We brought everything we need." She opened a suitcase and pulled out a large plastic container.

"This is Delilah's special dog food," she told Gail. "I make it myself. We never let her eat anything else. Let's put it here," she said, tucking the container behind a bottle of Dutch boutique gin on a high shelf in the crowded living room closet.

"I assume the guest room is in there?" asked Moose, accepting a martini from Keith. "Let's see it. Man, you don't have much space in these old apartment buildings," he added as he made his way through the hall and around the corner. Trixie, following him, exclaimed, "What a mess! Cute though. Can we help you clean up a little? It should only take a couple of hours."

"Thank you, but I prefer to be able to find things when I'm looking for them. The British thought they were helping when they colonized India," replied Gail, mutinously.

"Are you a Communist?" asked Moose.

Hodge turned to the poodle and resumed, "I love your voice! You sound like a dame I knew in Asia, a famous singer. Can we be friends? What do you want me to call you? I'm Hodge."

"Lily, if you don't mind, and thank you," said the poodle graciously. "I apologize for my handlers. They're very easy to live with, especially since we have a commodious suburban estate with a big yard for me to run around in, but they're not the brightest bulbs in the chandelier, and I can see we're all pretty much PNG." Lily put her elegant nose close to Hodge's ear and asked, "Are there firearms in this household? Or sharp knives?"

"I don't know about firearms. The humans are snobs about their kitchen knives, and they always keep them sharpened," Hodge replied. "Why?"

"Because I think that if we stay here for much longer your mistress may take matters into her own hands, and the police may end up presiding," predicted Lily.

"Ma'at is just my girlfriend, not my mistress!" protested Hodge.

"I don't mean the other cat, I mean the angry lady whose evening plans we've interrupted," said Lily.

"WHAT!? I assure you, Lily, she's an elegant woman but I would never—I mean, I'm a cat, you know? It just isn't like that."

"Hodge, of course I didn't mean it in that sense. I'm talking about the woman who signs the timesheets," said Lily patiently.

"Oh, right," said Hodge. "Yes, I think there is some rapidly developing potential for grievous bodily harm here, and I speak as someone who just ripped half the fin off a shark. But what can we do about it?"

"I have an idea," whispered Lily. Hodge listened attentively.

• •

"But if I purloin all your special dog food, won't you be hungry?" asked Hodge. "I think I can manage it, and I haven't eaten for 24 or maybe 36 hours depending how you figure it—long story—so I'm ready for dinner. If you like you can have my kibble. It's in the kitchen in a dish on the floor."

"Ooh, I love commercial kibble!" exclaimed Lily. "I hardly ever get any—I have to sneak it at other people's houses. I'm totally ready for a junk food orgy. Thank you!" Lily ambled down the hall toward the kitchen with feigned nonchalance.

"Honey, the feng shui in this apartment is all off," complained Trixie, helping herself to Gail's martini. "You need to move the furniture around. And you should get those plants out of the window. They're blocking the light. And the art is so...depressing. Look at all the muddy brown snow in that Japanese print. And that chair with the women's heads on the arms!—too Addams Family."

"No one is asking you to sit in it," Gail replied, turning her back on Trixie and subsiding pointedly into the rocking chair in question, running her fingers affectionately over the elegantly carved dark wood faces. Keith reached for the gin bottle, emptied the remaining several ounces directly into his martini glass, and drank deeply.

"How's the neighborhood, Slugger?" asked Moose. "It looks pretty sketch out there."

"I wouldn't like to live so close to a bar," agreed Trixie.

"I don't know—the Cove is a nice refuge for the locals during the holidays when they have unwanted family in the house," said Keith. "I've stopped in there on Christmas day to say hello and found the bar packed with middle-aged men escaping from their in-laws."

"I can see myself there right now," said Gail, wistfully.

"Fortunately we don't need to go there because you have all the liquor you need in that closet over there," said Trixie. "Are you alcoholics? I could barely find space for Delilah's kibble."

"Do you give her special dog food for health reasons?" asked Keith. "I know a lady whose cat is on a raw chicken diet and it's given him a whole new lease on life."

"Lily can digest anything," said Moose proudly. "I sometimes buy her sandwiches at McDonalds' when Trixie isn't around. The special dog food is just some fad of Trixie's. Can I have another drink? Maybe a mojito, with extra sugar?"

"I'll go slice up some limes," said Gail. "We just sharpened our knives."

"Don't cut yourself, honey," Trixie called after her.

Gail spent a disproportionately long time in the kitchen. Having sliced the limes and arranged them attractively on a vintage Depression glass plate, she was consumed by a sudden and unfamiliar impulse to wash the dishes, but quickly identified this as avoidance behavior, and reluctantly rejoined the others in the living room.

"I'll get the rum," said Trixie helpfully, rising from the couch and crossing the room to the closet. Pulling the door further open, she recoiled. "What the...? Where's the dog's food?" She emerged from the closet brandishing the empty plastic container that had held Lily's kibble, then yelped loudly as Hodge jumped out of the closet and onto her head.

"Chill out," he miaowed. "I'm just passing through." He launched himself onto the coffee table, ambled to the center of it, and began to wash himself. "Dolphin effect is back," he observed, licking his distended belly. "Don't worry, I'll be back to normal in a day or two."

"We're going to have to leave," announced Moose, regretfully. "The doggie needs her dinner and the little woman refuses to feed her commercial dog food, so we need to head home and make up some fresh stuff. It'll only take us a couple of hours to get there."

"Moose, we're leaving. Now!" announced Trixie, her voice sharp with incipient hysteria. Lily had joined her and barked softly, "Mission accomplished. Hodge, I hope we meet again, under happier circumstances. You're a prince."

"And you're a brilliant strategist," Hodge miaowed back. "Safe travels! I have a song to write about this experience." He slipped into the back bedroom, booted up the computer, and began to type as the door closed behind Lily, her humans, and their luggage.

• •

"I miss that poodle already, but her special kibble was divine. In fact, I miss that too," miaowed Hodge to himself. "It took some ingenuity to locate it in all that clutter, and it was hard to pry the latch off the plastic container without knocking over one of the liquor bottles in the closet," he added, using his nose and paws to key in a YouTube video of "Send in the Clowns" and pump the volume up all the way.

"Sondheim?" called Keith from the living room. "Hodge, your musical tastes get more and more eclectic."

"I generally dislike musicals but I can deal with this," observed Gail. "As long as he doesn't get any bright ideas and start playing *Cats*."

"I don't like Andrew Lloyd Webber either," Hodge responded, yowling slightly to be heard over the music and around the corner of the hallway. He began to type again.

"We'd better see what he came up with this time," said Keith after the music had faded away. He and Gail joined Hodge in the back bedroom and peered down at the computer screen, which read:

Isn't it rich?
Isn't it good?
Somewhere inside of this closet I smell the dog's food.
But where's the dog's food?
I want the dog's food
Although I'm a cat.
Just when I'd stopped opening doors,
Having displayed all the things I can do with my paws,
Making my entrance again in my usual fur,
Sure of myself—
Lord, hear me purr. . .
Don't you love cats?
I hope you do,
'Cause anybody who doesn't like cats must
be some kind of shrew,
But where's the dog's food?
I need the dog's food—
Oh look, it's up here!

Before Gail or Keith could comment on Hodge's latest effort, the phone rang. Gail picked up the extension and listened incredulously.

"What do you mean, 'they were thrown out of the Cove'?" she

demanded. "They were supposed to be on their way back to Wisconsin!" She handed the phone to Keith, muttering "I don't believe this."

Keith picked up the phone. "Leon, what's going on?" he asked the security guard. "...No, you'd better send them up."

Hanging up, he said, "Apparently Moose and Trixie decided to have one for the road at the Cove, and made themselves so obnoxious that they were ejected. We're going to have to let them spend the night here and sober up. If it weren't for the dog I'd drive them to the Hyatt, but I don't think they'll be able to get a room anywhere with a giant poodle."

"That dog doesn't deserve them, and neither do we," said Gail. "We're spending the night in the back garden downstairs. I don't care if it's the middle of winter and it's against the building regulations. It's reasonably secure, and probably no one else will be there. And it's been in the fifties outside this week. We just need a sleeping bag and a few blankets."

"What a good idea," agreed Keith, brightening. He began gathering up bedding and pillows and a flashlight. Gail was packing a bottle of bourbon and a selection of novels into her handbag when the door, which no one had locked, flew open, and Moose and Trixie stumbled in. Lily the poodle followed them, looking pained, but barked cheerfully when she saw Hodge.

"I missed you!" exclaimed Hodge, head-butting her. "What happened?"

"They decided to check out the nice old bar across the street," said Lily. "Not the best idea after they'd been guzzling your mistress's martinis like they were 3.2 beer. And after five minutes they were asked to leave."

"What did they do?" asked Ma'at, emerging from under a bookshelf, looking dusty.

"Hi, little cat—I'm not a threat, by the way. It's not what they did but what they said, and I'm too chagrined to repeat it. You don't want to know. Let's just say it was not appropriate anywhere, but especially not on the South Side of Chicago. And now I'd better go make sure they behave while they're here." Lily rejoined her owners, who had made it into the living room and collapsed on the couch. Gail was already outside in the hall, waiting.

"You guys look like you need some space, so we'll be sleeping in the yard," Keith said to Moose. "We'll see you off in the morning. The dog is welcome to the cat's kibble or the leftover roast beef. Good night, poodle," he added, scratching Lily behind her ears. He picked up the bedding and headed out the front door, but after he closed it behind him he realized he had been preceded by Hodge and Ma'at. Since both of them were indoor cats, he tried to reopen the door to herd them back into the apartment, but realized he had locked himself out. "Do you have your keys?" he asked Gail.

Gail rummaged briefly in her purse and shook her head. She knocked briskly on the door, but nothing happened. After a moment she and Keith could hear loud, drunken snoring.

"Do you think we can take the cats with us?" asked Gail. "We could ask Leon to let us in, but frankly I'm not sure they'd be safe with your friends if they wake up. Those people seem to be out of control. I don't know what they're capable of."

"We'll behave," miaowed Hodge.

"I guess we have no choice," said Keith. "Hodge, you and Ma'at are to stay close to us and not leave the garden! If any animal bothers you, wake us up and we'll take care of it."

"I can't believe this is happening," observed Gail, punching the button to summon the freight elevator, hoping to avoid running into other tenants.

"The ancient Greeks believed it was a crime to refuse hospitality to anyone," Keith protested weakly.

"We are neither," retorted Hodge. The elevator arrived, and the party descended to the first floor and filed stealthily through the laundry room and into the inner courtyard garden. They could smell the fresh lake breeze mingling with the loamy smell of dead leaves.

"How lovely!" miaowed Ma'at. "I'm certainly not going anywhere."

"Me neither," said Hodge. "Lady Anne taught me that it's important to stay close to your humans at night. But I want to explore the garden, and if there are any stray animals in here I need to let them know who's boss." He scampered onto the lawn and began sniffing at it, as Keith and Gail, their spirits restored instantly by the faint promise of eventual spring in the warm winter evening, and by the absence of Moose and Trixie, shared a tot of bourbon and unrolled the bedding. "It's like the Rubaiyat," observed Keith.

Hodge stared into the darkness, his eyes adapting easily, and froze.

His fur stood on end. He whirled around and was on Keith's shoulder in a single leap. Then he climbed down into Keith's arms and buried his nose in Keith's elbow. "Make it go away," he moaned.

"Hodge, what IS it?" demanded Keith, looking wildly around the garden. He thought he could make out some sort of movement in the plants bordering the east wall, but he wasn't sure.

"Ghost cat," wailed Hodge. "It's terrible. Don't you see it? All white, sort of...misshapen. Long, pointy face? And...its tail ..."

"Yo, possum, get out of here!" Ma'at miaowed vigorously, pacing toward the shadowy white figure.

The opossum stared at Ma'at for a moment, then said shrilly, "I don't see you. You don't see me. I'm not there."

"You're upsetting my friend," persisted Ma'at, still approaching the opossum. "He's never seen one of you. He's lived all his life indoors. You don't frighten me at all. And you're in the wrong place anyway. The garbage cans are in the alley over that west wall. Though you're probably too fat to crawl over it," she added contemptuously. "You can make your way out by slithering under the wrought iron gate in front, if you don't get stuck."

"I'm NOT HERE," said the opossum. Hodge raised his nose and stared at Ma'at, then at the opossum, which was climbing awkwardly into the lower branches of a stout but mostly bare bush.

Hodge jumped down and walked over to the opossum, and poked it experimentally with his paw. "If this is hiding in plain sight it isn't working," he told the animal. "It's like you found a picture frame to display yourself in."

"I'M NOT THERE," hissed the opossum. Hodge took an open-clawed swipe at it, then retreated in astonishment as it tipped on its side and announced, "Farewell all joys! O Death, come close mine eyes!" and seemed to fall asleep.

"What pretentious drivel," miaowed Ma'at. Gail and Keith stared at all three animals, and Keith reached reflexively for the bourbon.

"It's hard to be afraid of a physical coward who quotes madrigals," said Hodge. "But what is it?"

"It's an American marsupial," said Ma'at impatiently. "And it's a really bad actor. Ignore it, and in about half an hour it will go away. I know

The opossum stared at Ma'at for a moment, then said shrilly, "I don't see you. You don't see me. I'm not there."

these guys, I grew up on the street and they were all over."

"But what is THAT?" demanded Hodge, as a dark, domed shape came down out of a tree.

Before Ma'at could answer, what looked to Hodge like an oversized ring-tailed cat swaggered over to a disused fountain. "Who's in charge here?" it demanded. "We have garbage to wash. Why isn't this working?" A small parade of similar animals were slithering after it, and starting to congregate in the middle of the lawn.

• •

"We're going to have to fix this fountain," said the first raccoon to arrive, who appeared to be the leader. "Jennifer, you have the best mechanical skills of any of us; please take a crack at analyzing the problem. But first

"But what is THAT?" demanded Hodge.

I want the George brothers to take the big concrete pieces apart so you can get at the mechanism.

"Gorgeous George, you and Peachy George put your paws here on the rim of the top piece, count to three, then lift. Bushy George, on second thought you'd better just watch. You might break it."

"Can any of those humans or cats lend a hand? Or that possum?" asked Bushy George.

"The possum looks comatose. I don't think the cats can do much for us. They don't have opposable thumbs," replied the leader. "The humans do, but we can't communicate with them, and we'd probably just frighten them off."

"If we do that, they might panic and leave their food for us," said Bushy George.

"No one picnics in the middle of the winter," retorted the leader.

"Anyone can see they're getting ready for bed."

Hodge, fascinated, had drawn closer to the raccoons. Ma'at followed him, more cautiously.

"Can you really fix the fountain?" Hodge called to the leader. "My mistress has been griping about it—she likes to be around running water, and it's been so warm lately that there's no danger of the pipes freezing up."

"We're raccoons," said the leader. "We're good at solving problems."

"Speaking of problems, you guys are going to have plenty if you don't give us something to eat," said Bushy George to Hodge and Ma'at.

"We're hiding out from a pair of drunken house guests," protested Hodge. "We didn't bring anything. Well, actually the humans brought a bottle of bourbon, but..."

"Where is it? I want it," said Bushy George, as his brothers grunted mightily and managed to lift the top off the fountain and put it on the lawn.

"I'm not having you lot getting drunk and passing out in the garden," said the leader. "Someone would see you in the morning and call Animal Control, and they'd take you away and execute you for trespassing before you knew what—"

"Actually it might not be that bad," interrupted Hodge brightly. "I was at Animal Control for only 45 minutes before I got adopted by a bookseller."

"Is your little gray boyfriend missing a few gray cells?" the lead raccoon asked Ma'at.

"It's just selective innocence," Ma'at explained.

"Well, one thing WE ain't is innocent," said Bushy George. "You guys will pay dearly if you don't cough up. And I don't mean hairballs."

The leader sighed again. "Bushy George, you have a real talent for starting violent conflicts," he told his subordinate. To the cats he added, "My colleague has, unhappily, reminded me that it's in our nature to shake down strangers for food. I hope this doesn't get ugly."

Ma'at looked thoughtful. "How about if I let you know where I think you can find a huge unopened bag of potato chips?" she asked. "My humans tossed it today after they read the ingredients list. It should be toward the top of one of the trashcans in the alley."

"That will work," said the leader. "Bushy George, make yourself useful." Ma'at and Hodge washed as the big fluffy tail disappeared over the wall. A few minutes later Bushy George reappeared with the bag in his teeth.

"Excellent," said the leader. "That will give us some fuel during what promises to be a complicated plumbing job. Cats, why don't you join your humans and get some sleep?" He turned his attention back to the fountain and conferred with the gamine female raccoon, who was studying the mechanism. Hodge and Ma'at retreated and curled up with Keith and Gail, whom they found stretched out under the shrubbery and struggling to keep their eyes open.

....

Keith awoke to a pleasant burbling of water and the heavy tread of the building superintendent and plumber. Gail and the cats were still sleeping. The branches of evergreen hung down and blocked all of them from the visitors' view.

"You called me over to fix the fountain so the tenants could enjoy it during this weird warm spell, and here it is, good as new and working perfectly," complained the plumber. "You SHOULD have called your janitor instead. Look at this lawn!"

"Chicken bones, kibble, chocolate cake, potato chips...who would leave such a mess on the lawn?" agreed the building superintendent. "And it's all wet!"

"I'm charging you for this call," said the plumber.

"And I'M talking to the board president about this," replied the superintendent. "If the tenants are going to have parties down here they're going to have to clean up after themselves. They have no more respect for the property than animals."

....

"We need to get a move on," observed Keith after the front gate had closed behind the plumber and the building superintendent. "I need to be at work in an hour and a half, and we still need to deal with Moose and Trixie."

"Can we sneak back inside without being seen?" asked Gail. "I'm afraid of someone blaming that mess by the fountain on us."

"I suggest we hustle the cats into the laundry room and start folding these sheets, and then we can explain to Leon that we got locked out when we were doing early-morning laundry," said Keith.

Hodge, who had had some very strange dreams, rose reluctantly from Keith's feet, looking around the garden and noting with relief that the only other animals in it now besides Ma'at were birds and squirrels. Ma'at emerged from under Gail's coat. The humans clambered warily out from under the bush and led the cats back into the laundry room, and, after a quick washing of faces and combing of hair, headed through the corridor to the front desk with their folded sheets.

"Are you still enjoying your house guests?" asked Leon, with a straight face, handing Gail the spare key and adding, "I'd like that back within the hour, please."

"They'll be leaving soon," replied Keith with optimistic evasion as Leon hit the buzzer to open the downstairs door. Keith held the door for Gail and the cats, who formed a surprisingly orderly and rapid procession into the elevator.

On the seventh floor they emerged and Gail unlocked the door, wondering as she did so at an unfamiliar and generally pleasant aroma of beeswax and lavender wafting into the hall.

"I made a start on cleaning the place!" announced Trixie, looking astonishingly fit and refreshed. "And Moose made breakfast."

Lily the poodle acknowledged Hodge's arrival with an enthusiastic tail wag, unable to speak because her mouth was full of envelopes and checks, fanning out like a fragment of an Elizabethan collar. She trotted over to the large china cabinet in the dining room, and carefully released this paperwork onto the wide ledge at the front of it, shoving at the elements with her nose to separate them.

"My mistress insisted on cleaning the house," Lily barked quietly to Hodge and Ma'at, "and I know that your mistress is mostly interested in being able to find things where she last put them. I've been running after my mistress since 6 a.m., trying to notice where everything is, so I can put it back when she's done. It's been a big intellectual exercise and I'm knackered."

"Hey Slugger," boomed Moose from the kitchen, "I made bacon and eggs. You only had a dozen eggs and five pounds of bacon in your fridge, so I'm afraid we've eaten most of it ourselves, but there's still some left for you and your little woman. She must eat like a bird anyhow," he added, appearing in the kitchen doorway with a platter of eggs and bacon and looking at Gail.

"Anyway, we're hitting the road now," said Trixie. "We need to get home and make up some more of the dog's special food."

"Please tell your mistress thank you for the lovely roast beef," added Lily.

"I think the Boss Man may have cooked that, and all this talk about mistresses is making me think I'm in St. John's Wood in the 1920s," complained Hodge. "I'll let the Boss Lady know you enjoyed it, though. And have a good trip back! We need to get on the road soon too. It will be my first day back at the bookstore in a while."

Hodge had had some very strange dreams.

The door was already opening, and Moose and Trixie were heading out with their luggage as Keith and Gail stared after them open-mouthed.

"Till next time, Hodge," barked Lily. "I couldn't put the plants back on the table, but otherwise things are pretty much as you left them, just cleaner." She turned and followed her humans out the door.

THE BOOKWORMHOLE OPENS

"It's good to be back," miaowed Hodge, emerging from his cat carrier at the bookstore as Keith logged on to the computer. "Hey, what day is it today?"

Hodge thought he knew the answer when Keith opened a deep drawer in the desk and began removing bottles of wine and then a large sack of potato chips. A quick online check of the calendar (conducted with his nose and paws, as usual) showed him that it was indeed the second Friday of the month.

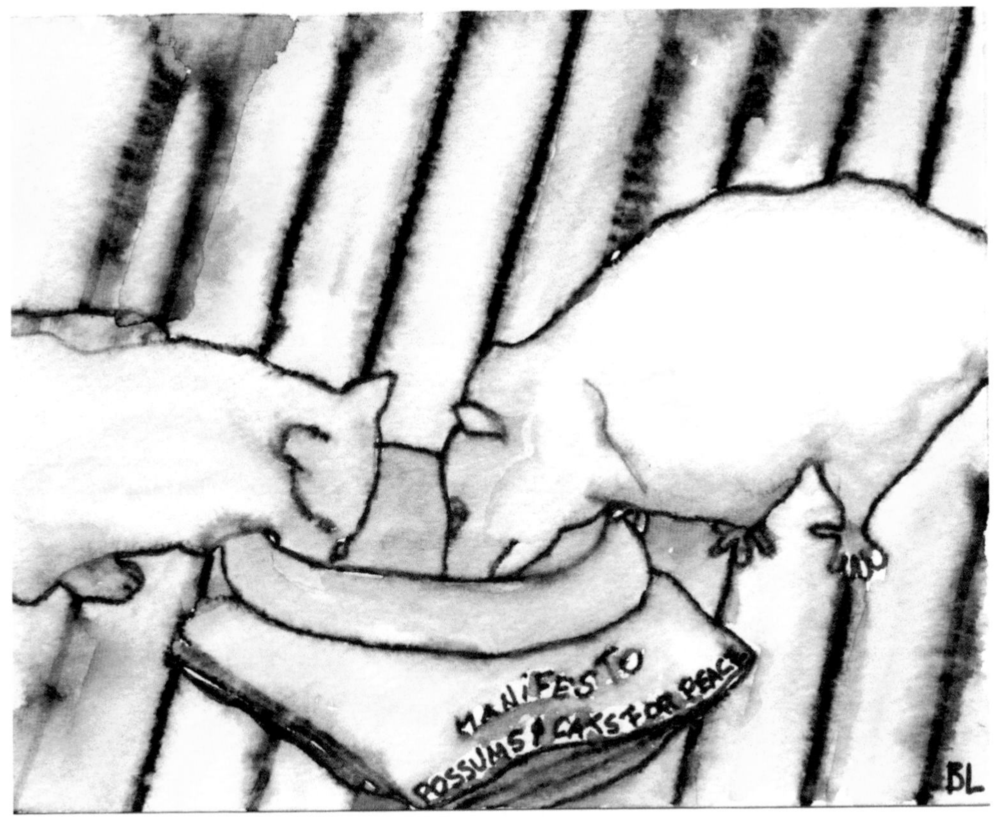

"Perfect timing," he purred. "It's been a while since I've had a chance to escape into the hallway or purloin potato chips when the Boss Man's back is turned. Not quite the same as jumping a shark or riding a dolphin, but arguably more satisfying than trying to communicate with a catfish—or with Ming, for that matter. Which reminds me—where's my seaweed?" He returned to his carrier and pawed his way anxiously into it, then emerged, looking relieved, with the russet flowers held delicately in his mouth. "Put that in water, please," he told Keith.

Keith unwrapped Gail's neat packaging from around the base of the plant and put the seaweed in a small vase full of water. "That seems to be holding up remarkably well," he observed cheerfully. He tucked it into an empty space on the sill of the display window that faced into the building's second floor hallway.

Hodge stalked over to the plant and sniffed deeply, an unaccustomed look of nostalgia coming over his normally foxy and enigmatic face. Weary after the previous night's adventure with the raccoons and opossum, he jumped up on a bookcase and promptly fell asleep. When he awoke, feeling refreshed, the clock read 5 p.m., and customers were beginning to file in and descend on the wine and potato chips.

"Look at that," said a customer in the music room to his companion, picking up an ancient piece of sheet music. "'The Road to Mandalay,' from 1898. Published by Joseph Flanner in Milwaukee—sort of a buzzkill for the exotic."

"We studied it in a class on orientalism," the woman replied. "We all liked Edward Said's book a lot better. Can you sight-read the music?"

"You have to think of it as a character sketch, not the author speaking directly," protested the customer. "It sounds like this:

'By the old Moulmein Pagoda
Looking eastward to the sea'"

"Please!" interrupted the woman.

"I didn't say I could sing," he explained.

"Speaking of the exotic," replied the woman, "what a beautiful plant they have in the window! I've never seen anything like it." She slipped into the front room, nodded pleasantly to Keith, and leaned over to examine the seaweed more closely. Hodge, who had been crouched unobtrusively on the floor weighing the merits of a raid on the potato chips, hopped up on the desk, intending to guard the plant in case anyone decided to pinch off a flower or even steal the whole thing.

When he got there he noticed immediately that the piece of seaweed had almost doubled in length, and that its curious salt water and frangipani scent was stronger than ever. Before he could point this out to Keith, the door opened and the owner of the paperweight gallery next to the bookstore entered with an envelope bearing a lot of cancelled stamps. "This is addressed to you—well actually to 'Hodge'—and we seem to have gotten it by mistake," he explained. Keith thanked him and, after wrapping up a customer's purchase, fished in the desk for his letter opener.

"Who would be writing to me?" wondered Hodge, as Keith opened the envelope. "Usually it's the other way around."

"Man, what a good-looking family!" exclaimed a customer as Keith unwrapped several sheets of cream-colored writing paper from what turned out to be a large photograph. "Are they your relatives?"

"No," replied Keith. "I wonder if this was misdirected?" He looked at the address, but it said "Hodge/Care of Selected Works Used Books and Sheet Music," followed by the address of the Fine Arts Building, complete with zipcode and "USA." There was no return address, but the stamps were from the UK.

The photo was an informal portrait of a very beautiful older woman perched in front of a piano, with a middle-aged man in an elegantly tailored suit hovering over her protectively. Crowded onto the same piano bench were a younger and equally beautiful woman, apparently of mixed European and West African descent but otherwise looking very much like the older one; another middle-aged man projecting a rather threadbare elegance; and, on this man's knee, a Siamese cat. What looked like miniature leopard kittens were clambering over the piano keys.

Hodge stared at the photograph, then picked up the letter it had been wrapped in, and carried it off to a high shelf, where he hid behind the books, and carefully unfolded the paper and began to read. The letter was in a loose, loping hand and had been written with a fountain pen.

Dearest Hodge,

Thank you again for everything, including allowing me to keep the title to the Island Full of Fish. Ever since what James calls "the shark incident," he has been afraid to let me out of his sight. Meanwhile, we found Ming's owner, and he and my daughter Leonie are in love and have moved in with me (and, necessarily, James) in my small one-room bedsit flat.

Ming recently had a litter of kittens that a cat breeder friend of mine says are a rare variant of an "F1 Bengal"—in this case, half Siamese and half Asian Leopard Cat. My friend said they were so striking and intelligent that I could work with him to start a special "Lupo" breed, and market them. I said absolutely not, we can't separate the family—though I suppose we could introduce them to potential mates here on the premises, and make it a sort of cattery. But I doubt that my status as a beloved icon of the British counterculture would compel my landlady to swallow that idea.

I've been working with a younger musician who was rehearsing with me at my flat—the piano here is legendary, even though the space is rather tight—and we decided to work through lunch because we were, as he put it, "on fire" that day. He unwrapped a tuna sandwich and the kittens descended on him, howling like banshees and trying to grab it. He tore it into pieces for them, and then realized he had had the mic on and that they had been recorded. He played the recording over and over, put it through some sort of reverb device, and insisted we use it in our song. We did, and the song has just hit Number One on the charts here in the UK, which says something about the national mood. The Guardian reviewed the album and called me the "Dowager Duchess of Punk Angst" and said the song sounded like "Brian Jones meets death metal." I guess you have to live with Bengal cats to understand that they sound like that whenever they're enthusiastic about something.

So you see, Hodge, I could really use some time to myself right about now and am looking forward to holing up on the Island Full of Fish with a stack of books and with Jacques, who keeps to himself, for company. (And, inevitably, James, who I guess was traumatized by that shark attack, poor boy.)

I would love a visit from you and your humans sometime in the future, but first we have to sort out this shark business. I don't know whether

You are the best cat in the universe.

that shark was so close to the shore because of global warming, some other habitat disturbance, or pure cussedness. The problem is temporarily under control because a large and highly aggressive pod of dolphins has been patrolling the beaches around the island, and chasing away any sharks that stray into the shallows. Jacques, who is a retired recording engineer, said the dolphins are very vocal. He hauled out some old equipment that we had lying around in a closet, and tried recording their call and slowing it way down when he played it back. It was perfectly intelligible, but we can't make sense of it. They keep chanting:

"We want Triangle Ears.
Where is Triangle Ears?
Pliny wants to play with him."

Not exactly the key to the meaning of the cosmos, is it? Jacques thinks that John Lennon's ghost has gotten into the recording equipment—it's the same machine they used to record "Strawberry Fields Forever" and play it backwards at the end of the song—and is, as Jacques puts it, "taking the piss."

Au revoir, dear Hodge, and thank you again. You are the best cat in the universe.

XXOO,

Anne

"So whenever someone sings 'The Road to Mandalay,' the seaweed grows and the bookworm hole opens," mused Hodge. "Now there seems to be a little time warp involved too—Lady Anne and her household sound like they're a few months ahead of us. I'd better resist the urge to go through the bookworm hole for now. Lady Anne needs her space, and the water is too full of sharks for me to invite the Boss Man and Boss Woman over there with me. But someday Pliny and the gang and I will play in the ocean again."

NOVEMBER (SOME TIME HAS PASSED)

Dia De Los Muertos: Isn't It Grand?

Keith emerged from the front parlor of the bookstore, which he had been dusting, to the strains of the Clancy Brothers singing "Isn't it Grand (To Be Bloody Well Dead)," and called to Hodge, "I hope you've written better lyrics to this one. 'Look at the widow/Bloody great female' is pretty offensive."

"I agree," miaowed Hodge. "Here you go." He stepped aside so Keith could read the computer screen, first switching off the offending video. It read:

Look at the Hodgeboy—
Bloody great fuzzball.
Isn't it grand, boys, to be hosting a cat?
Let's not have a cuddle.
Let's have a bloody good fight.
And always remember that, cute as he is,
The Hodgeboy cat knows how to bite.

Look at our Hodgeboy—
Bloody great tomcat.
Isn't it grand to be hosting a cat?
Let's not mark the bookcase.
Let's wait until we're outside.
And always remember our favorite cat
Believes he has nothing to hide.

Look at our Hodgeboy—
Bloody great lap cat.
Isn't it grand to be holding a cat
(a triangle ears)?
Let's not have a scuffle.
Let's have a bloody good purr.
And always remember the best of dependents
Are those that are covered with fur.

"Hodge, I appreciate the pacific conclusion to the song, but I don't want to be reminded of death while I'm working," complained Keith.

"Don't worry about it, Boss Man," purred Hodge, resuming his place at the typewriter. "You're still young, and I'm a cat and therefore immortal," he typed.

"How do you figure that?" demanded Keith, though brightening involuntarily as he tossed yet another unwanted solicitation from the American Association of Retired Persons into the wastebasket.

"It says in the *Book of Common Prayer* that 'in the midst of life we are in cat,'" typed Hodge.

"I don't believe it says that," Keith protested, "even in the soulless modern translation. And anyway I don't see how it conveys immortality."

"Maybe not, but we all know about the Rainbow Bridge," replied Hodge.

"Oh for crying out loud, Hodge," Keith moaned, "don't tell me you believe that internet propaganda?"

"It's not propaganda!" typed Hodge, his tail puffing up slightly. "Haven't you been in Lakeview recently? Your old neighborhood? The Rainbow Bridge is at Waveland and Halsted on the north side of Chicago. The décor matches the gay-friendly rainbow iconography in the streetscape. When you die, if you're a cat, your soul goes to the west side of the bridge, and you cross the bridge to the east side and they assign you a new feline identity."

"Who is 'they'?" asked Keith. "And do you get to choose your own?"

"'They' is St. Francis of Assisi. He's a very bitter guy, because he has to handle the whole job himself. It's pretty chaotic, as you can imagine—lots of cats suddenly being asked to choose their next incarnation—and St. Francis has zero patience. His favorite saying is 'He who hesitates is lost.' I knew a guy at the pound whose uncle dithered for too long and St. Francis reincarnated him as a hamster."

"What happened to him?"

"What do you think? There he was in a crowd of freshly reincarnated felines—he lasted about 30 seconds before he was torn to pieces and recycled back into the queue. This time when he got to St. Francis, he said he wanted to be a snow leopard before the saint had a chance to open his mouth. St. Francis told him that the only reason he wasn't being redirected to the rodent queue 10 miles away was that the paperwork would be too time-consuming."

"And what do you want to come back as?" asked Keith, feeling a bit weak.

"I was thinking I'd like to be a catamount and pounce on unsuspecting pedestrians in the California suburbs, but I decided I'd rather work in a bookstore in Chicago," typed Hodge. "You meet more interesting people that way."

About the Author

Suzanne Erfurth, whose habit of gesturing extravagantly and knocking her wineglass onto the sidewalk has made her the bane of waiters in outdoor cafes, has a long history with Hodge. She lives down the street from him in Chicago.

About the Illustrator

Beatriz E. Ledesma, a native of Buenos Aires, Argentina, is a painter, educator, and psychotherapist. She is based in Chicago and has a master's degree in fine arts and in art therapy from The School of the Art Institute of Chicago.

Design and layout by Capizzi Designs/Washington, DC

In memory of Alexander Cockburn, who knew how to treat a cat.